Sisterwood

A Novella

By Kathryn Vigness

Book design by Erika Alyana S. Duran

ISBN: 979-8-218-52103-5 (Paperback)

First Edition

Chapter 1

"Have you heard anything from Margo?" Gwen asked as she entered the kitchen.

Betsy scoffed. "What do you think?" she replied. The cupboard door creaked open as she grabbed two mismatched coffee cups and clanked them onto the laminate countertop. "Of course, I haven't heard from her. I've only left a million texts and voicemails."

Sad, but true, Betsy thought. She had been keeping Margo up to date on everything that had transpired with their mother as if Margo was involved but couldn't make it to the phone. Meticulously detailed messages and voice texts went unanswered and every day, Betsy continued to follow up with more information from their mom's care team and her severe decline. Betsy wasn't sure if it was more for Margo or herself, sending these messages. Margo had made it clear by her silence that she wanted nothing to do with their mother or her end-of-life care, yet Betsy felt it was important that Margo be kept informed.

Betsy made her way around the spruced-up but still outdated kitchen with its painted cabinets, resealed Formica countertops, and black appliances that desperately needed a wipe down from last night's—hell, last month's—supper splattered across.

The house was a "fixer-upper" that Betsy and her husband Jake bought right after marriage. Their initial plans were to renovate it completely and use the equity to buy something to grow into. The joke was on them because a month after closing, a terrible storm blew through and the beautiful elm tree that Betsy had adored in the driveway was now on their roof. Shortly after, Betsy found out she was pregnant. All their money went to fixing the roof and making their temporary house a home. The remodeled bathroom and kitchen Jake had promised were figments of his imagination. Betsy looked around and realized they were still eyeball deep in this fixer-upper—12 years later.

"I tried calling her," Gwen said, her voice soft and almost kid-like. Betsy turned to look at her sister. "She didn't answer, obviously, but I thought maybe, just maybe, she'd answer if she saw it was me."

Gwen's demeanor had shifted and for a slight moment, Betsy swore she caught a glimpse of the twelve-year-old, doe-eyed, gangly girl who used to appear at the supper table every night after their dad died. Jake knew when he married Betsy that Gwen was a package deal. Lucky for them, Gwen became like a big sister to their kiddos because the last place she wanted to be was home, alone. So every night like clockwork, Gwen would enter through the back door and find herself at the kitchen table, first for supper and then for homework.

Gwen, the bright and bubbly extrovert who earned her way through university on scholarship, who just graduated from Michigan State with her bachelor's degree in journalism, and who was now breaking her back trying to make a name for herself as a journalist for the

Lansing State Journal, looked at Betsy the same way she did over two decades ago. Full of innocence and defeat.

"Gwennie-girl," Betsy said in a soft tone, using the nickname she gave Gwen when she was born. "You can't save everyone." Betsy sighed as she watched Gwen's face crumple before she caught herself and corrected back into her stoic, poised self.

Betsy knew deep down that was the type of person Gwen was. Gwen saw injustices everywhere and tried so hard to combat them. In high school, she was a devoted volunteer with the Special Olympics, ran for Student Council, then Student Government, and was on the debate team. All of this on top of being captain the volleyball team and in the National Honor Society. Everyone who knew her growing up figured she was going to be a social worker for underprivileged youth.

When Gwen had decided that journalism was where she was going to make the biggest impact, Betsy was surprised. "Are you sure this is the route you want to go?" Betsy had asked.

"Bitty," she replied, using her pet name for Betsy, "this is how I can give a voice to people. I can listen, tell their stories, and be an advocate for them. I can create change by reporting on it and shedding light on all the noble causes that are out in the world, but we just never hear about them!"

"I'm not trying to save everyone," Gwen said now. "I just thought maybe Margo would pick up if it was a call from me."

"We can't just wait around for her," Betsy said. "We've let her know that mom is gone. It's up to us to figure out the rest."

The spurt and gurgle of the coffeemaker had just finished, and Betsy rose to fill both mugs. She pushed over stacks of papers, bills, and medicine pamphlets that covered the kitchen table to make room for both to sit, but a few spilled over onto the floor.

"Let me get that," Gwen crouched down to pick them up and shuffled them neatly onto the corner of the counter. As she turned back to sit down, Betsy grabbed the funeral home's folder with scribbles of Mom's last wishes completed in it. Well, last wishes that they thought she wanted, at least.

It had been less than twenty-four hours since their mother had passed, but it had been close to two years since she was lost to Alzheimer's disease. And two decades since the first symptoms had appeared. By the end, their mother, Susannah, wasn't able to recognize them or hold a full conversation. Her lucid days were few and far between, but in the rare moments of clarity, Susannah was her jovial and exuberant self the girls remembered her as.

It was shortly after Gwen was born, when Betsy was ten years old, and Margo fourteen, that Dad and the older girls noticed something was off with Susannah. Innocent things like her forgetting about picking Betsy up from the mall or what time Margo's basketball game was, or swearing she had made supper only to find out she was remembering yesterday.

Susannah passed it off as a joke, laughingly referring it to her "mom brain" being all over the place. At ten years old, Betsy didn't know any different. She was just happy when her mom did remember to pick her up before she scrounged a quarter to call from the pay phone multiple times because her mom never answered.

It had gotten particularly worrisome when Margo and Betsy came home from the cabin on a Sunday night. It was a miserably hot stretch of summer and Gran had brought the older girls up for the week to stay by the lake while Dad was away for work. In the midst of all the teenage things like pouring Sun-In in their hair and lathering up with baby oil to lay out in the sun, days were filled with swimming in the lake and hiking through the woods. At night they would canoe out on the water with Gran just to see all the stars shining above the treetops.

Betsy remembered this trip because on the last day, one moment she was laying in the hammock reading a book and the next she woke covered in mosquito bites as well as a raging sunburn. In response to her wailing, Gran told Betsy to jump in the lake to cool down. They slathered her in pink calamine lotion to ease the sting after drying off. Betsy remembered that miserable ride home, hours in the station wagon with her head against the window, watching the trees flit by in her peripheral vision. She counted the telephone poles, for she willed herself to wait for every 10 poles before she could itch. "I don't want to hear another word about an itch," Gran warned. Betsy knew well enough not to make a fuss.

Betsy and Margo had opened the front door to the house, dumping all their bags, pillows, and blankets as soon as they entered. Betsy saw Gwen sitting alone at the bottom of the stairs, pacifier in her tear-stained face and a saggy diaper. She perked up when she saw it was Margo and Betsy. Gwen toddled over with arms up wanting to be held.

"Jesus," Margo hissed. "Where is she?"

Betsy reached for Gwen, "Gwennie-girl," she cooed. "What's the matter? Shush, shush. I'm right here." Betsy held her close, and Gwen's silent, hot tears streaked her face and neck.

"Nana?" Gwen's big eyes searched Betsy's. "Nana?"

Confused, Betsy said, "No, Gran went home, but I'm right here." She cuddled Gwen close again.

Gwen shifted, sliding out of my arms and down to the ground, running towards the kitchen. "Nana?" she said, pointing to the brown bananas on the counter.

"Are you hungry, Gwennie-girl? You want a banana?" Betsy asked.

"Yeah, yeah," she replied. Her pudgy, dimpled hands clapped.

"Hmmm, those bananas look icky. How about an applesauce?" Gwen squealed as Betsy opened the pantry to look for an applesauce cup, but realized there were none. "Sorry, Gwennie-girl, no applesauce either. Let's see what else we can find."

Gwen's bare belly gurgled and Betsy turned to look at her fully. At twelve, she had taken the certified babysitting course, although she had been watching Gwen since she was born two years prior. For almost two years Betsy had been mothering this sweet girl as if she were her own. As Betsy stood back and had time to take the full sight of Gwen in, she realized that Gwen had food crusted in her hair, her diaper sagged as if it hadn't been changed all day, and when Betsy glanced over at the couch, Gwen had her favorite stuffies lined up.

Betsy reached for the graham crackers and asked, "You want some of this?" Gwen squealed with delight. Betsy hoisted her onto the counter and broke one in half. Gwen greedily grabbed both halves and started gnawing away.

Margo came into the room and seethed. "I think Mom left her here all day!"

"What?" Betsy asked, trying to comprehend. "She didn't leave Gwen. Are you sure she's not upstairs?"

"No! I went through the entire house!" said Margo.

"So where is she?" Betsy asked. "It's after supper, she should be home."

"I don't know!" Margo exclaimed. She was getting more agitated by the minute. At the age of twelve, Betsy didn't quite understand what the big deal was. Mom left them home alone all the time.

"Mom leaves us home alone all the time," Betsy's voice echoed her thoughts.

Margo whipped around to look at Betsy, "Yes, Mom leaves *us* home all the time. But Mom doesn't leave *Gwen* home alone!"

That's when it hit Betsy. Her sweet, beautiful Gwen, home all alone. *What was she thinking?* Betsy thought. Just then the back door opened up from the garage and Susannah burst through.

"Girls! You're home! I'm so glad to see you!" she exclaimed.

"Mom!" Margo barked. "Where were you? You left Gwen home. Alone."

Confusion ran over Susannah's face. "Left Gwennie home?" Her eyes darted across the kitchen to Gwen on the counter in front of Betsy holding the graham crackers. A horrified look came over her face as her hand flew up to cover her mouth. "I left Gwennie at home!" She ran over and started smothering Gwen with kisses and hugs, embracing Gwen with every fiber of her being. Betsy heard her murmuring into Gwen's downy hair, catching every other word of *I'm sorry* and *never again.*

"Where were you, Mom?" Margo demanded.

"I...I was out," Susannah stammered. "I got up to go to church this morning and the ladies wanted to go for brunch and then I ran a few errands and I just lost track of time!"

"Didn't you know Gwen was even home?" Margo yelled again. "What were you thinking?"

"I...I don't know! Maybe I thought she was at the cabin with you?" Susannah replied. "I don't know what I thought. How could I forget my beautiful baby girl?" She continued to sway as she held Gwen tightly.

It was at that moment that they all knew something was wrong with their mother. Even at the age of twelve, Betsy knew her mother would never intentionally forget one of them or do anything to hurt them. But to have just witnessed a whole day of not remembering she had a toddler at home?

Susannah made an appointment with her doctor for the following week, which was the beginning of years of doctoring. Every few months, there would be an uptick in symptoms, but then the next day she would be fine. Susannah would blow it off as if the symptoms the day before were an anomaly and that she was perfectly healthy. Symptoms like a sudden onset of confusion that included memory loss, and being awake and alert and knowing who she was despite memory loss. Scans showed no signs of damage to any particular area of the brain, so she didn't have very specific problems, such as being unable to move an arm or leg, uncontrollable movements or problems understanding words. Doctors were perplexed.

This went on for years until signs started to show on the regular. Susannah couldn't remember a change in plans, such as meeting times changing or a change in location. She was confused about time and place. Or had difficulty with familiar tasks. The doctors eventually labeled it as Transient Global Amnesia. The episodes of memory loss were severe countered by days, even weeks of complete normalcy. One Thanksgiving not long after Dad died, Betsy and then-boyfriend Jake came over on Susannah's insistence of hosting the meal. Betsy had begged her mother to let her help with the cooking to try to relieve some stress, but Susannah insisted she could handle it. When Betsy and Jake had arrived for their 1:00 p.m. sharp dinner call, Susannah not only had forgotten to turn on the oven, but she couldn't remember how to mash potatoes. Betsy found her mother flustered and disheveled in the kitchen, unsure if she had already put in the milk and butter or not, and trying to ask Google.

Symptoms finally escalated to Susannah having her license taken away because she would get in the car and forget where she was driving. Twice Betsy had gotten calls from state troopers asking her to come pick her mom up, once as far as three hours away. When asked where she was going, Susannah said she had an errand to run but forgot where it was or what she was getting. For close to two decades Betsy and Gwen had watched their mother slowly decline before doctor's ultimately diagnosed Susannah with Alzheimer's disease only two years after Betsy and Jake's marriage.

That was the beginning of the end. Margo never responded to Betsy's messages and Gwen was still in elementary school, so Betsy became her mother's executive power of attorney. She and Jake eventually took Susannah in to care for her full-time until that became too much. "I'm just your old maid," Susannah used to joke when she was in a lucid state, cleaning up her dishes after supper.

Susannah lived in the nursing home for the past year, but it had been two years since she last recognized who Betsy was. Susannah knew she had three daughters and loved telling stories of how beautiful and accomplished they all were. How Margo lived in Chicago and worked at one of those big buildings down in the Loop. Or how smart Gwen was for getting a scholarship through college. Or how her Betsy lived a good life right here in Harrison and how she hoped Betsy would visit soon.

Betsy sighed as she opened the folder of Mom's last wishes. "I guess it's time to say goodbye," she said.

Gwen reached her hand across the table and grabbed Betsy's. "We already did."

Chapter 2

Margo bustled off the L train, shaking off the crisp wind that blew through the throngs of people determinedly trying to get home after a long day at work. She hurriedly passed through the vast outliers of all types of people who ride the L. Businessmen and women who are mentally running through their caseloads. Teens with large backpacks who either are just getting off practice after school or headed to work for a shift before bed. Elderly folks slogging through the wake of people, in no particular hurry as the long night alone awaits them. Mothers pulling their kids' hands along trying to catch the next track to make it home in time for the bedtime rush.

Even with the biting breeze cutting across her face, Margo's body thrummed from the high of closing that big client account this afternoon. FreshHarbor, a food and beverage distributor, expanding out of the Midwest and into national chains, accepted her marketing proposal that she had pored over for the past six months. This was her first big client acquisition as the lead Strategic Accounts Manager. Her team had worked tirelessly over the past few months locking everything into play to seal this deal, and while she should be out celebrating—the team headed out to O'Hennessy's after work—Margo couldn't wait to kick off her pumps, pour herself a big glass of chardonnay, and sink into her deep tub to steep in essential oils and listen to her favorite playlist, newly dubbed on Spotify. She promised herself that when she landed this deal, she was going to start taking better care of herself. Still slightly buzzed from the bottle of champagne they popped with the client at the office, Margo relived her big win and barely noticed the crowds of people around her.

Maybe I should've gone to O'Hennessy's with the team, Margo thought. *Show them I'm a team player? Then again, Morrison never showed up when he was the lead.* The crowd filtered down to just a handful of pedestrians as Margo turned the corner onto the street where her highrise sat. *Well, if he did show up,* she thought, *it was because he was a creep not wanting to go home to his wife.* Margo pulled open the door to her building and felt the familiar rush of warmth and vanilla sea salt that permeated the lobby. That smell was the first thing that attracted Margo to her building. Not just the stellar downtown location and the 1930's prewar architecture, its unmatched view to the north and south of Chicago from her living room, or the beautiful rooftop where she dreamed of hosting parties one day. Sure, those were the details that officially sold Margo on this co-op, but it was the hint of vanilla sea salt that enveloped her every time she walked into her building. It reminded her of a simpler time. A small piece of her childhood that she longed to remember.

Margo hit one of two buttons in the elevator and moments later, the doors opened, and she stepped into her expansive view of Chicago. The setting sun cascaded golden hues throughout the apartment. The generously high ceilings offered more depth and the rich mahogany floors glistened in the sunset. Within a few steps into her home, she was flooded with a spectacular view of the harbor, lake, and city skyline.

Margo glanced around the immaculate apartment. "Maria sure can do wonders," she muttered. Maria was her assistant who came once a week but quickly became Margo's right-hand woman. Even though Margo lived alone and spent more time at the office than she did at home, Maria kept the household running smoothly. She stocked the fridge with nourishing, easy-to-grab foods for Margo to eat on the go. Maria watered the houseplants and stacked the mail on the counter, separating it into junk, bills, and follow-ups. Maria washed, folded, and put away the laundry and even emptied the dishwasher. Margo only ran the dishwasher once or twice a week, but not having to empty it was a task she thoroughly appreciated not having to do. Margo quickly noticed that had Maria washed the windows as the setting sun was extraordinarily exquisite tonight.

"I love freshly washed windows," Margo had said to Maria when hiring her. "I want to be able to see the stars when I look out at night. That's very important."

Margo had hired Maria about six months after the divorce. Margo quickly realized she couldn't, or maybe simply didn't want to, do it all. By throwing herself into her work, Margo was able to not focus on the mess that her personal life was.

She had met Brett at an after-hours work party. He was a senior partner who worked in Acquisitions, and she was a new hire in Marketing. What started as an innocent encounter quickly turned into a fling. Margo found herself sneaking off to his corner office during work hours or catching a late dinner after he was done with his meetings. From there, it quickly became something hot and heavy. A fresh—and secret—romance with a man fifteen years her senior became her kryptonite.

It was Brett's idea for Margo to fly to New York City with him to attend a conference. Margo could enjoy the city while he attended meetings and hosted meet-and-greets for clients, but she would be his plus one to dinner parties and evening social events.

"I'll pay for everything," Brett said. He knew Margo's paycheck wasn't even a third of what he made as a salary. Margo's pride, however, wouldn't let her go overboard. Her Midwest roots of living within her means still held true. Even in the 'big city' of Chicago, Margo couldn't shake the push and pull of wanting to fly but knowing she should stay grounded.

Oh, but she loved the idea of living a life like Brett. Not having to live paycheck to paycheck like she did during college or even now. She had enough to live comfortably, but if her car got wrecked or they jacked up her rent, she would be back to living like a college student again. But Brett was living the dream. He had a car service pick him up in the morning. He had a cleaning service. A corner office. People in the company loved how he played hardball—and usually won. Margo didn't see that side of Brett when they were alone, but she did catch glimpses of it when he was with colleagues. The gregarious laugh, pointed humor—usually at someone else's expense—and the look. Brett had a demeanor about him that came out in negotiations and his colleagues dubbed it the look after one particularly hard acquisition client wouldn't budge on the terms of their deal. Brett had them locked in a corner and they both knew it. Brett just had to wait for the client out. And he did, but while he waited silently, Brett stared the client down with his steel gray eyes. When the infamous deal finally went through, the look became just as infamous.

After a late night of partying with colleagues and acquaintances at a national conference in NYC, it was Brett's idea to elope.

"Let's get married," Brett said. He was breathless as he kissed her passionately.

"Married?" Margo asked. "Here? Are you crazy? We've been together for less than a year!"

"I don't want to wait anymore!" Brett exclaimed. He had a wild look in his eyes. "We're good together. I don't want to sneak around. I want to wake up with you in my arms for the rest of my life!"

Margo melted into him.

"Margo," Brett said as he got down on one knee. They were in the middle of the sidewalk, somewhere in the Upper West Side. It was well after midnight. "Will you marry me?"

A huge smile spread across her face. She nodded, her response barely escaping her lips. "Yes!"

Brett wrapped his arms around her as they kissed under the streetlight.

The next morning, they skipped the conference and went to City Hall to inquire about obtaining a marriage license. Per New York State law, they only needed to wait twenty-four hours after acquiring it, so they spent the day shopping and dreaming about their new life together. First, they had an appointment at Atelier Eline to pick out a princess-cut 2-carat solitaire diamond with a matching 2-carat wedding band. Margo had forgone the traditional dress route and instead found the perfect, vintage white pantsuit in the East Village while splurging (an entire paycheck!) for white leather Christian Louboutins adorned with crystals.

Brett stopped at Bergdorf Goodman's for a suit fitting. Luckily, he was a standard size 38 jacket which needed minimal alterations and could be done in-house. Lastly, they stopped by a flower vendor in Greenwich who promised them she could make an arrangement and open her shop early the next day so they could pick up the flowers on the way to City Hall.

The next morning at 9:30, they stepped into City Hall. Fifteen minutes later, they were husband and wife.

Looking back, all the red flags were there; however, at twenty-four years old, Margo was too infatuated with Brett to identify them. She was head-over-heels in love. Maybe if she had listened to her roommate Hattie when she saw Brett out with another woman. Or maybe if Margo had trusted her gut when she overheard remarks by other women in the bathroom stalls at some of the events she attended. Or if she asked more questions about his past instead of taking it at face value.

Or maybe none of that would have made a difference.

Regardless, for as smart as Brett was as a businessman, he didn't have Margo sign a prenup. He thought he had a compliant wife, but soon learned otherwise. Margo was not tolerant to the lies Brett cast. When their marriage dissolved due to "irreconcilable differences"—Brett was a lying, cheating, man whore who knocked up his partner's secretary—Margo won a fine settlement in the divorce. Which she used to promptly buy her co-op on North Lake Shore Drive and eventually hired Maria to take care of her personal life since Margo wasn't to be trusted with it quite yet.

A slight smile spread across Margo's face as she noted all her favorites waiting for her by the tub. A chilled bottle of chardonnay in the ice bucket, her favorite wine glass with the gold stem, her playlist already playing from the speakers in the bathroom, and all the goods to make her bath simply divine.

Margo sank into the tub once it was filled, the scents of lavender and chamomile filling her nostrils. She closed her eyes and inhaled deeply, letting the water support and release her. After a few breaths, she indulged in a deep drink of wine. The mix of the hot water and the continued buzz from the day lulled Margo into a happy stupor. She finally picked up her cell and opened the main screen. She had turned off all notifications long ago and hadn't heard her phone audibly ring in years. She couldn't even remember what her ringtone sounded like. She scrolled through messages of congratulations and laughed at the memes sent in her team's text thread. What she wasn't prepared for was a message that popped through as she was holding her phone. A message she knew was coming but couldn't possibly brace herself for.

"She's gone."

Chapter 3

Gwen pulled her hair into a messy ponytail as she pored over her research. She was sitting at her desk, humming along to the playlist she dubbed "WRITE" on Spotify to distract her from the chaos that reigned around her in the newsroom. It was only 2:00 in the afternoon, but editors were already approving layouts for tomorrow's edition of the *Lansing State Journal.* She had submitted her piece and was now plugging away on the research for her first big byline—one she pitched last week. It was a story near and dear to her heart; funding for the Special Olympics was being jeopardized in legislature. Gwen was adamant about raising awareness, showcasing the underbelly of the policy changes and economic factors state legislatures tried to portray versus the advocacy and awareness needed to keep programs like the Special Olympics running across the state.

When Gwen first started as a beat reporter, Betsy couldn't wrap her mind around the fact that Gwen wanted to be a journalist.

"I don't know how you do it," Betsy said. "Always running around trying to get the next best story before anyone else. Newspapers are dying! If anything, at least social media and television break the news in real time! Here, you're always a day late!"

"I just want to be able to tell people's stories. Social media and TV reports are 30-second blurbs primarily used for click-bait. I want to write—to get to the heart of the story and fill it with feeling. Plus, every day is different, which thrills me," Gwen replied.

It was Gwen's first official journalism class in her junior year of college that sparked her interest in writing instead of reporting. She had zero interest in being in front of the camera, even though she had the face for it. She was tall, on the slender side—but toned thanks to many years of yoga—with moody hazel eyes and a beautiful wave of chestnut hair. The instructor's first writing assignment piqued her curiosity about the power of writing.

"Your first assignment is to report on something challenging in your life right now," he said to the classroom. "Do not just give facts about how tired you are or the immense workload of a college student. Go beyond that. You can certainly give those facts but dig deeper. How does the lack of sleep affect classroom performance? Or what are the correlations between a heavy workload and college graduation rates? Interview peers and talk to professors. Or write about something personal. Relate it to the reader. Even if it doesn't directly affect them, how does your writing persuade them to relate to the story?"

Gwen chose to write about Alzheimer's Disease and how it becomes a family disease, not just a patient's disease. She pored over facts and researched psychology and sociology studies about the effects on family dynamics and even cultural differences when taking care of a person with Alzheimer's. She had firsthand experience with her mom and although she was living an hour and a half away, Gwen knew the toll it was taking on her sister Betsy, who had been their mom's primary caregiver since Dad died.

When her instructor handed back their assignments, a green sticky note was on her copy with the words "office hours" scribbled across it. Terrified that she had somehow failed after putting so much effort into the paper, she sank lower into her seat and didn't bother to engage in the conversation, but dutifully took rigorous notes instead. After class, she waited roughly ten minutes before mustering up the courage to knock on her professor's office door. She heard a gruff, "Come in," and she gingerly entered.

"I had a note on my paper to come see you," she said. Her voice ended her sentence more like a question.

"Ah, yes, Ms. Hampton," Professor Julien said. "Please take a seat." His office smelled like a damp closet. Musty books filled the shelves—anything from classic literature like *Catcher in the Rye* and *Don Quixote* to the newest AP Style Manual to a severely used thesaurus thrown gruffly back on the shelf.

Gwen slid her backpack off her shoulder and took a seat in the green faux marble vinyl chair that faced the professor's desk. She observed his demeanor, noting how he pushed his round, tortoise glasses on top of his salt and pepper hair and left them askew. He relaxed back into his office chair, hands on the worn, padded handles. The buttons on his navy, button-down shirt stretched with him, and Gwen hoped they were sewn on tight.

"I didn't want to make a fuss about this in front of the whole class," Professor Julien started. "But I want to commend you on the excellent paper you handed in."

Gwen exhaled a breath she didn't realize she had been holding. A deep rush of relief spread across her.

"The exposé on Alzheimer's Disease with a personal touch on how it affects the entire family is exactly the kind of journalism I was hoping for. It was well thought out, well researched, well cited, and quite honestly, one of graduate level work," he continued. "It takes a lot for an old guy like me to get excited over twenty-year-olds writing hard-hitting stories, but you have something here. A knack for well-rounded writing."

Gwen sat dumbfounded in her seat. She stammered out a meek thank you, but the vinyl she was sitting on made an egregious noise as she shifted uncomfortably, so she decided to keep quiet.

"Our next assignment coming up next week is similar to the assignment you just did. However, instead of picking your own topic, I'd like to give you one," Professor Julien said. "I want to see how well you can take an obscure topic that you may not be intimately familiar with and see what you make of it. I'm giving you an extra week's notice than the rest of the class, so you can do with it what you will."

"Okay," Gwen said, her voice still somewhat lost.

"There's a unique opportunity I have in mind for you," he continued. "Normally I have graduate students who can fill this role, but this year's students are..." he waved his hand dismissively. "Meh."

He smiled. "I'd like to take a chance on you instead. It's a paid writing position on my staff for an online publication, *InsightGlobalOnline.* We cover more in-depth interviews and stories on complex social justice issues. If you can do the same level of work on this next assignment as you did on this past one, the job is yours. If you want it, of course."

Gwen's vinyl chair made another terrible noise as she shifted yet again. "Yes, of course," she replied. "I will do my best!"

"I have no doubts," the professor responded. "I can see you're a rising star! If this assignment lives up to your last, consider yourself hired!"

That was her first big break. After she completed the next assignment, Professor Julien used it as an example in front of the rest of the class. He then emailed his staff editor to onboard Gwen and that was the start of her journalism career. She also planned to go on to grad school thanks to Professor Julien's encouragement. She hoped to collaborate with the Sociology Department on her thesis regarding the societal impact on caregivers for patients with Alzheimer's.

So it came as a blow, personally and professionally, when Professor Julien left Michigan State as a tenured professor, but also left his job at *InsightGlobalOnline*. New management came in and unfortunately, it didn't matter how good of a writer Gwen was, they restructured and let go half of the staff.

Looking back, Gwen had felt protected by Professor Julien when she worked at *InslightGlobalOnline*. Now, as a newbie at the *Journal* with an editor not much older than her, but with a bigger attitude, Gwen felt the pressure to live up to her experience. Yes, her resume was one of a veteran journalist, but the job market was tight and after so many rejections of being overqualified for entry-level jobs and underqualified for experienced positions, Gwen took the first offer that came her way: a salaried position that barely paid her rent, required long hours with few benefits, and included an uncovered parking spot on the fourth floor of a four-story parking lot.

At least it's a writing job, she thought. *It could be worse. I could be a receptionist with a bachelor's degree.*

Gwen checked the time, something she had been doing roughly every fifteen minutes. She had one last meeting at 3:00 and she'd be on the road by 4:30, she calculated mentally. Gwen made the hour and a half drive up to Harrison multiple times a week these days while staying most weekends at her sister's house. Her social life was nonexistent, as her days consisted of work and nights consisted of either driving or being on the phone with Betsy.

Mom hadn't been able to recognize them for almost two years now. First, she couldn't recognize a picture of Margo, then it was Gwen, then she couldn't recognize the woman in the mirror, but lastly, and most heartbreaking, was not recognizing Betsy. Once it became too exhausting for Betsy and Jake to continue to care for Mom, they decided to place her in the nursing home. Betsy still went daily to visit, and Gwen whenever she was home, visited, as well. However, Gwen knew those days were numbered. Her mom's care team warned it was a matter of time now.

Gwen took another drink of her now-daily habit of afternoon coffee from the shop down the block in the Capital building. Gwen's go-to these days has been a Capital T Latte, their cutesy name for an overpriced sugar-free toffee flavored latte.

Her phone buzzed next to her computer and a notification popped up. *Message from Betsy* it said. She picked up her phone to read:

It's happening. Come home.

Gwen swept up her things, grabbed her laptop and coffee, and shouted to Leslie next to her, "I've got to go. I'll call my 3:00 and ask for a phone interview instead. I might not be in tomorrow." Leslie, a friendly and calming presence in the office, nodded. Gwen kept her up to date on her family drama and Leslie kept Gwen up to date on her dating drama. It was a win-win for both of them.

Gwen took a painfully slow elevator to the top level of the parking garage and ran to her car, parked at the far end. It had seemed like a good idea to park her new car away from other vehicles so as not to get door-dinged, but that backfired today. Her car beep echoed through the garage as she unlocked it. It didn't take long, and Gwen was on the road, exiting toward US-127 headed north.

I should call Margo, she thought over and over again. Each time the thought intruded into her head, she talked herself out of it.

Forty miles down the road, she muttered, "Screw it."

She dialed Margo's number and waited.

Chapter 4

Betsy and Gwen were seated in the conference room of the funeral home; the folder filled with loose-leaf pamphlets spread out in front of them. Betsy couldn't help but notice how the muted beige walls blended with the muted tan chairs with wood grain armrests and the unremarkable carpet.

I wonder if that's on purpose. Everything here is unremarkable so as to not detract from the present moment. Forcing families and loved ones to make decisions while in grief.

John, the funeral director, continued to drone on about different aspects of arrangements when Betsy interrupted him. "None of this matters," she said. John bristled as he stopped talking. Even Gwen was taken aback by Betsy's abrasive tone.

"What?" Betsy challenged. She shifted forward in her chair causing the spring to creak, filling the room with an unpleasant sound. She took a deep breath. "What I mean is," Betsy continued in a softer voice, "Mom wouldn't have wanted us to sit here and have some cookie-cutter funeral. Just because she couldn't remember what she wanted doesn't mean she didn't know what she wanted."

John shifted uncomfortably in his chair. He cleared his throat and asked, "And what is it that your mother wanted?"

Betsy remembered why she didn't like John. He was a local who went off to college in Wisconsin and recently moved back home when his funeral director father decided to retire after forty years. Back in high school, John was three years ahead of her and a know-it-all. He was a nice kid, but Betsy saw right through his façade. John was one of those people who said all the things he thought you wanted to hear instead of listening. Betsy remembered how Margo sneaked her into a party when she was sixteen and John was there.

As the night went on, his stories got more and more obnoxious as he boasted about getting out of this town and all of the culture and nightlife college had to offer. One of the guys Margo hung out with clocked him because he wouldn't shut up. John didn't come home much after that, Betsy remembered. Not until he moved back to take over his family's business.

Betsy looked John over. She didn't like the worm-like, bushy mustache that sat atop his thin mouth. It did not distract from the abnormally large pores that dimpled his nose. The color of his green eyes popped from the shade of green in his tie, but his suit jacket was much too large for his frame. *He should really invest in a tailor,* she thought.

"Mom wanted to be cremated," Betsy said. "And we don't need any fancy urn or a headstone." She rifled through those pamphlets and put them off to the side. Gwen looked at her with a curious face. Betsy explained, "After Dad died, Mom had enough presence of mind to tell me what she wanted. It was a bit jumbled, but I did take notes to piece it together. She wanted to be cremated and for us to spread her ashes in the lake. She did specifically mention fall when all the colors were most vibrant."

"The lake?" Gwen repeated.

Betsy sighed and nodded. "I mean, I have no idea if she meant Lake Michigan or any of the other 12,000 lakes we have around here, but that's what she said."

"According to state law, there is an ordinance restricting where ashes can be spread," John replied. "If I could interest you in Package D..."

Not missing a beat, Gwen piped in. "That won't be necessary, John. I think that part is settled. Let's move on to the service."

Betsy bit the inside of her bottom lip to hide her smile. She didn't give her Gwennie-girl enough credit when it came to sticking to her guns.

~~~

An hour later, Gwen and Betsy walked out of the funeral home with a plan. Five days after that, they would hold a service for their mother. No pomp and circumstance. No massive floral spreads in white. No
~~~

blown-up portrait to say goodbye. It would be a simple, yet beautifully intimate ceremony of family and friends celebrating the life of their mother.

Gwen had been driving back and forth from Lansing every day, making it a three hour round trip. It was in those miles alone that she grieved for her mom. For herself. And just like when she was a child, she found solace in Betsy's presence—a nurturing, strong, and stable force that Gwen needed to breathe at times. But she never felt like she could break down in front of Betsy. Gwen knew Betsy was holding everything and everyone together like she always had. So Gwen used those highway miles to let the tears fall unabashedly, for by the time she reached either Harrison or Lansing, whichever direction she was headed, she had cried all her tears and was ready to put on a strong face.

Stories of Susannah were shared over the course of the week leading up to the funeral. Their next-door neighbor, who the girls referred to as Aunt Lee, sent a note of condolences. A newspaper clipping from 1993 was tucked neatly inside. It was an article about the donation of 500 books to the elementary school when Susannah was the President of the elementary PTA.

"I forgot all about this!" Betsy chuckled. "We had boxes and boxes of books all over the dining room! Books kept coming and eventually they covered the table and then every single chair and all over the floor. For like two weeks, we had no place to eat supper, so Mom pretended we were having a picnic in a different city every night and we'd look up facts about the city in the encyclopedia! It was something like spaghetti in San Diego, pizza in Philadelphia, mac and cheese in Miami, chicken in...Cleveland or something like that."

Gwen laughed as she envisioned their mother serving chicken nuggets on a blanket in the living room. "Why Cleveland?" she asked.

Betsy chuckled, "I have no idea. I think she ran out of places and just said the first thing that popped into her head. I just remember that one because Cleveland wasn't in the encyclopedia."

The day of the funeral, Susanna's sister, the girls' Aunt Eliza, delivered a beautiful eulogy. Susannah and

Eliza had been close their entire lives. Susannah cooed that Betsy was named after Eliza, and Eliza mentioned that anecdote in her speech. She remembered Susannah as a creative and imaginative child, a loyal friend, and devoted mother, showing up as best as she could for her three children. Eliza made note that it was hard to watch her graceful and humble sister deteriorate cognitively over the course of her lifetime, but her spirit never faded.

Both Gwen and Betsy spoke on behalf of their mother. They shared tidbits about their childhood and how they shielded those who didn't know the extent of their mother's disease until later in life. Through the tears, everyone chuckled at how Susannah was ruthless when it came to board games or cards. After the doctor told her to keep her mind sharp by playing with her girls, Susannah took those orders seriously. "She never let me win!" Gwen said.

Simple memories were some of the most poignant, like how Susannah hummed while doing tasks like cooking or cleaning. Her distinctive laugh: a high-pitched noise followed by a snort. How she always ate after everyone else. Her love for decorative tea towels and fancy soaps. How their house was filled with vanilla sea salt, Susannah's favorite scent. How children were drawn to Susannah and how she was robbed from enjoying her grandchildren because of how quickly she was fading.

As the service went on, Betsy tried to sneak a look at those who filled the chapel within the funeral home. She gave a small smile when she made eye contact with a relative before turning back to the minister. Conflicting emotions had bubbled up to the surface all week. Sorrow for losing her mother, but gratefulness that she was no longer suffering. Exhaustion from years of holding everything together, compounded by debilitating guilt over the sense of relief that it was over. Heartache for her two kids who never knew the grandma they were hearing about today, yet at peace knowing they loved their grandmother all the same. But mostly, Betsy felt a gnawing grief of her own life unlived while she had to take care of so much at such a young age. Who could she have been if she didn't have to raise Gwen and take care of their mother while Dad worked? What if Dad hadn't died so suddenly? What if she wouldn't have gotten married and pregnant so young and could've finished college? Betsy's entire life from the age of fourteen on had revolved around caring for everyone else except for herself.

As the service finished, Betsy felt as if she was floating, almost as if an out-of-body experience. She stood as guests filed up to give their condolences to the family. On autopilot, she shook hands, said thank you, and gave half-hearted smiles. Next to her was Gwen, looking as melancholy as she felt. But in that high above, floating sphere, Betsy confirmed what she already knew.

The chapel in the funeral home was modest, but for a town the size of Harrison, it seemed ample. Through the gathering of people, one person was noticeably absent.

Margo was nowhere to be seen.

Chapter 5

It had been three months since Susannah passed away. Betsy had gotten back into her routine with her job at the school, focused on caring for her two kiddos who had dual diagnoses of learning disabilities and ADHD. Most days she felt good about how they managed throughout the day together, but other days were rough. Days like when Dani didn't take her meds and was fidgety and interrupting nonstop. Or when Sam couldn't concentrate because he didn't sleep well the night before due to anxiety over the test that afternoon. Betsy provided frequent redirection for her kids on top of co-regulating their moods. Sometimes it was overwhelming. Today was one of those more challenging days that left her depleted and, try as she may, her family was not getting the best version of herself that night.

While grieving losing her mom had been hard, Susannah's passing was also a blessing. That juxtaposition of bittersweet left Betsy with insurmountable guilt. *How can I feel like I can breathe again not having to run over to the nursing home every day? She was my mother. I miss her. But also, I can finally be me again.* These thoughts swirled back and forth, over and over in Betsy's head throughout the day. Just when she thought she could move forward healthily, grief and guilt slammed against her.

It was close to dinnertime when Betsy came through the door, arms filled with grocery bags. She dropped her keys on the counter as she untangled her limbs from the plastic handles that left wide, red indentations on her forearms. Making multiple trips to the car to bring in the groceries was a chore, so she always challenged herself to try to make it all in one trip—milk included. *I knew I shouldn't have waited until tonight to stop at the store,* she lamented to herself.

As she turned to put the cereal and Pop-Tarts in the pantry, Betsy accidentally caught the edge of the bag and the remaining boxed contents spilled to the floor, along with the basket that held the mail. Annoyed, she hastily bent down to retrieve the boxes of macaroni shells and crackers to put away. She then scooped up the mail and quickly glanced through the contents. She mentally discarded the junk mail, but an official-looking envelope caught her attention. It felt thicker than the other mail, in weight and texture. It wasn't a cheap envelope that bills come in, but rather, official-looking stationery.

Betsy glanced at the return address: *Gorsnick and Associates, Attorneys at Law.* "What in the world is this?" Betsy said aloud. There was no one in the kitchen to respond. She quickly forgot about the groceries, opened the drawer to retrieve the letter opener, and sliced the envelope open.

NOTICE REGARDING ESTATE

On behalf of the estate of Susannah Hampton, who died on 5 July 2021, you are summoned to Gorsnick and Associates office for an official reading of the last will and testament on 18 October 2021.

The notice is mailed or delivered to you as required by law because the person who signed this notice has identified you as a spouse, heir at law, or beneficiary under a will of the deceased person named above. This notice is to tell you that, in the circuit court clerk's office, listed above, either a personal representative has qualified or a proponent has probated the deceased person's will. THIS NOTICE DOES NOT MEAN THAT YOU WILL RECEIVE ANY MONEY OR PROPERTY. The name, address, and telephone number of a personal representative or a proponent of the will is provided in the above letterhead.

Any questions regarding the above estate will be referred to the aforementioned time and date official reading. All beneficiaries have been notified.

Sincerely,
Maury Gorsnick
Gorsnick and Associates

Betsy read and reread the letter multiple times. "What will and testament?" she said. "Mom didn't have anything like this." Confused, she reached for her phone, hitting the last number that she had dialed. Gwen.

"Did you get a letter?" Betsy asked when Gwen answered.

"I was just about to call you and ask the same thing!" Gwen exclaimed. "What is this about? I thought you took care of all the legal stuff?"

"I did," Betsy replied. "Or I thought I did? I don't even know who this Gorsnick and Associates are." She flipped the envelope over and looked at the return address closer. "It says it's from Atlanta, Michigan. That's where Mom grew up."

Confused silence mulled between the two on the line.

"This is weird," Gwen said. "Do you think Mom had money somewhere that we didn't know about? Maybe she forgot she had?"

"I have no idea," said Betsy.

"Or maybe she had a baby way before us and gave it up for adoption and she kept the secret from Dad and then forgot all about it and now her death certificate triggered something, and we show up to the meeting and find out we have a brother!"

Betsy laughed in surprise. "You are way too into the news lately."

"Well, it happens! I just listened to a podcast that perfectly fits this scenario!" Gwen started going into detail about the synopsis of the series.

"I don't think mom had a kid without any of us knowing. But I guess we'll have to go up to Atlanta to find out," Betsy said.

The two hung up and Betsy hunched over the counter, staring at the letter, her mind racing with possible scenarios. Money. Land. Another family.

The oven beeped, signaling it was done preheating and effectively shaking Betsy out of her thoughts. Real life awaited.

~~~

Two weeks dragged by before Betsy and Gwen were driving north, both sipping on coffee on the way to Atlanta in Betsy's silver Chrysler minivan. Gwen had come up to Harrison the night before, crashing at Betsy's like she did for so many nights in the past year. To Betsy, it felt good to have her back home. Betsy noted how much she missed having her sister around. There was always an extra hand with meals or running the kids to practice or just to have an adult conversation. Jake worked so hard and was a great father and provider, but he was also gone a lot as it neared the end of construction season. Having Gwen stay gave Betsy the much-needed reprieve she needed.
~~~

Betsy and Gwen pulled up to the attorney's office, a plain brick building with maroon shutters and soffits. The greenery was well kept in front of the building, but looked a tad outdated, Betsy noted. *Arborvitae is the lazy route to landscaping,* she thought.

"Ready to meet your long-lost brother?" she joked as she put the vehicle in park.

"Ha ha," Gwen replied sarcastically.

"Maybe we can teach him the secret sister's choice handshake and everything," Betsy continued on.

Gwen rolled her eyes. "You're impossible. Let's go."

They walked in and were greeted by a middle-aged woman with funky, short hair, styled asymmetrically across her face with streaks of blonde and purple in the fringe. She stopped typing, pulled off her cat-eye readers, and smiled. "You must be the Hampton sisters. The other parties have arrived, so you can just follow me down the hall. You'll be meeting in the conference room."

The spunky gal motioned for them to follow her and as she turned, Gwen looked at Betsy with wide eyes and mouthed, "Other parties?" Betsy was just as bewildered and shrugged.

As they trailed down the hall, both Betsy and Gwen stopped short as they entered the conference room. There, sitting at the table with, presumably, Mr. Gorsnick was, in fact, their long-lost sibling.

~~~

"Margo!" Gwen exclaimed. "What are you doing here?"

Before Margo could answer, the older gentleman stood up and walked over to introduce himself. His kind eyes met Betsy's, though she wasn't sure if she could fully trust in what she was seeing.

"Ladies, welcome," he said. "My name is Maury Gorsnick, but you can call me Maury."

He shook both of their hands with a genuine smile. His hair was a soft gray—not quite white, but well on its way to becoming so. He dressed fairly casually for a lawyer, Betsy thought. Loafers, navy dress pants, a collared shirt under a cardigan, no tie. "Please, can I
~~~

get you anything to drink? Water? Coffee? Tea?" He gestured for them to sit.

"I'm good, thank you," Betsy said.

"Water," Gwen replied. Her voice was almost hoarse as if she hadn't used it in days. She couldn't keep her eyes off Margo.

They both took seats opposite Margo, and once Maury filled Gwen's glass with water from the pitcher on the built-in counter behind the table, he took a seat at the head of it.

"Well then," Maury starts. "I guess you're wondering why you're here." He paused before continuing. "It has come to my attention that your mother was a beneficiary of property. Now, I didn't know your mother, so when her death certificate came across my desk and I looked further into it, you three were labeled as her beneficiaries."

All three sisters were silent and stared at Maury. None of them dared to look anywhere else.

"It is my job to read you the last will and testament of your mother and to answer any questions you may have," Maury said.

"I was not aware that Mom even had a will," Betsy interjected. "I was her medical power of attorney after Dad died, and not once did anyone say anything about a will."

"Yes, sometimes that happens when people sign documents when they are young," Maury explained. "The original date of this will is May 2, 1973. That would have made your mother"—he shuffled through papers to find her birthdate—"just nineteen years old."

Betsy's look of bewilderment made Maury continue.

"Per the state of Michigan's law, I will read Susannah's Last Will and Testament out loud and then I can answer your questions." He cleared his throat as he pulled out the document.

Maury read the legal jargon in his best lawyerly tone. The words were dry and nondescript. Betsy tried to not glaze over. *Just get on to what it is that she left,* she thought. Out of the corner of her eye, Betsy noticed a fat, bumbling fly erratically hitting the window.

After a few minutes, Maury looked up at them to signal this was what they came for.

"I hereby bequeath any land and estate in my name to my children, should I have any. If I have no children, I deem this Last Will and Testament to be null and void and any land and estate will be subject to public entity."

Maury finishes by setting the paper down and taking a drink of water. He folded his hands and asked, "What can I clarify for you?"

"First of all, what land and estate are we talking about here?" Margo interjected.

"It appears that there is an estate not far from here," Maury explained. "According to Google Maps, it is a cabin on West Town Corner Lake?"

Margo and Betsy stared at each other from across the table. "The cabin," Betsy whispered.

"And when was this signed?" Margo asked.

"It appears that she signed this document on the same date that her mother, your grandmother, signed her will. Your grandmother bequeathed all her belongings to your mother and your mother bequeathed all her belongings to her impending children. It appears that Eliza and Susannah were both present at the original signing. There were no adjustments made until August 15, 1999, when Susannah updated the will to include three beneficiaries: Margo, Elisabeth, and Gwen."

"August 15, 1999," Betsy whispered. She looked to Margo to try to recall that date.

Margo exhaled loudly and sat back in her chair as if a strong gust of wind blew her over.

"August 1999, Bets," she said.

The realization hit her like a ton of bricks. Betsy's hands flew up to her face as she exclaimed, "Oh my god!"

Gwen, still lost in translation, asked, "What? What does August 1999 have to do with anything?"

"It was right after we came home with Gran," Betsy said, staring at Margo. "It was right after we found Gwen."

Margo nodded.

Gwen interjected, "Found me? Found me what?"

"She knew," Betsy said, shaking her head. "She knew something was wrong."

"Bets, what's going on?" Gwen asked. This time her voice sounded shrill.

"Gwen," Betsy said gently as she looked her sister in the eye. Betsy laid her hand on Gwen's. "I'll explain everything, I promise. But just give me a minute, okay?"

Gwen nodded. The three sisters all looked at each other, figuring out their next move.

Chapter 6

The three sisters stood outside of Maury's law office. No one said a word as they processed what had just occurred. The air was thick with questions; Margo shifting uncomfortably, Betsy fumbling for her keys, and Gwen wanting to say something—anything—to bridge the chasm between the three. The brisk wind scattered fallen leaves between their legs, settling in a bunch next to the berm. Shades of yellow, gold, and brown glistened in the late-morning light.

"So, I guess we own a cabin now?" Gwen said, breaking the silence.

Betsy looked up from her purse, keys in hand. "Oh Mylanta, Gwen. We are not keeping that place," she said. Betsy's face was filled with exasperation. "I will contact a realtor or someone to handle the sale. I doubt the place is even standing. If it is, a family of raccoons has probably lived there for more generations than us."

"What do you mean?" Gwen asked. Her tone voiced indignation. "I didn't even know about a cabin until—" she looked at her watch "—a half hour ago, and you have already gotten rid of it!" Her wild hair grew bigger blowing in the whirling wind. She shook her head, trying to tame it and keep it out of her face. "What is so wrong with that place? How do you know all about it? Why do you want to get rid of it? Tell me what's going on!"

Margo adjusted the handles of the designer tote slung over her shoulder. "She's got a point, you know," she said indifferently. "We don't even know what's left of it or if it's worth the hassle of selling."

Gwen smiled smugly at Betsy while Betsy gawked back and forth between her two sisters. *How did we get here?* she thought. *We haven't been together in years and now they're ganging up on me? Over this?!*

"This is ridiculous," Betsy finally said.

Gwen already had her phone in her hand. She held it up and said, "It's literally only twenty minutes from here." She cocked her head to the side and gave Betsy a look. "You're seriously not curious at all? To drive an extra twenty minutes out of our way?"

Margo chimed in, "I already flew all the way up here. I might as well drive over to see what we inherited. Then I can be done and get on with my life."

Rage overtook Betsy. She threw her hands in the air and shouted, "Get on with your life? Seriously? That's rich. *Real* rich. Haven't you gotten on with your life in the past...oh, I don't know...twenty years?"

Margo, her face without an etch of emotion, replied, "I am driving up there. You can join me or not. I would just like to see what's left."

Gwen stood as still as a statue, her eyes the only part that moved between the two. She let out a low exhale when she heard Betsy reply, "Fine."

~~~

The drive was silent. Gwen had the address mapped into Google, but not once did Betsy look at it.
~~~

Their route took them through the Atlanta State Forest and the rolling hills were filled with the perfection that only a Michigan fall would present. A high noon sun etched through the treetops, highlighting the deep beauty of reds, golds, greens, and browns. Steep curves outlined lakes and smaller, unnamed murky ponds. Leaves from the mature aspen and oak trees littered the roadway and ditches, while the silver, red, and traditional maple trees gracefully waved their branches as the sisters drove. Occasionally Gwen noticed an unmarked gravel driveway, but thanks to the coverage of the forest, farmsteads were blocked from view. She soaked in the beauty of her home state, for living in the city, she forgot how much she missed the simplicity of taking a drive in the fall.

Once they turned left onto County Road 622, the two-lane road became more desolate. The speed limit lowered to 45 miles per hour to accommodate for the steep winding roads. Curves cascaded over rocky terrain. Gwen looked in the rearview mirror and saw the sleek, black BMW sedan Margo was driving. *Surely a special request for the car rental,* she thought.

Betsy slowed down as they came up to a rickety old bridge. Gwen was amazed this was legal or safe to drive over. It was wooden, with horizontal, beat-up-looking beams to drive across, barely wide enough for one car to pass over, let alone meet another vehicle. The second would have to wait on the other side of the bridge until the first passed safely across. Gwen could hear and feel as the tires moved over each beam. She looked over the side of the bridge to a babbling creek. Boulders and rocks filled the edges, and she noticed moss growing on one side. She quickly inhaled as she spotted three deer—a doe and two fawns—drinking at the bank. As if right on cue, they looked up and ran off.

Not much further, Betsy took a right onto a gravel road heading north. Again, she didn't need Google Maps to tell her where to go. She knew. Gwen didn't question it but was genuinely curious as to how and why. So many things were left unsaid.

It wasn't long before she saw it. There, nestled into the woods, was a two-story, red-sided, wood cabin with a log front porch. Overgrown evergreen trees flanked the sides of the cabin. A huge red maple adorned the front and one hundred yards from the porch was a beautiful opening to a glistening body of water.

"Oh my god," breathed Gwen. "You've been here? You knew about this place?"

Betsy parked the car and sighed. "Some things you just want to forget about."

Gwen opened the car door and sprung out of the car. "This is magnificent!"

Car doors slammed. Margo and Betsy approached Gwen and the three stood shoulder to shoulder staring up at the cabin, soaking it in.

Though its grandeur and beauty were evident, so was the obvious decay. Shingles curled and spots where some were missing dotted along the roof. A screened window hung cockeyed on its hinges on the second story. Leaves accumulated in piles against the beams on the front porch, clearly stuck in gaps between uneven floorboards.

Margo was the first to break the silence. "Takes your breath away, doesn't it?"

"I can't even," Gwen replied. Questions gushed out like a geyser. "It's absolutely beautiful! When was it built? How long has it been in our family? How have I never been here before? How did I not know about it?"

Betsy interrupted Gwen's flow of questioning. "Let's just take a look around." She was lost in thought.

The women started up the path—Margo first, followed by Gwen, then Betsy. The front porch echoed with the clicks of their shoes and boots. Margo reached for the handle and the door popped open easily, but not without a groan and a crack in response. As Gwen found herself inside, she looked around at a spacious living room already furnished. She recognized the outline of two chairs and a sofa that was covered in old sheets. Books lined a bookshelf next to the tall stone fireplace that spread across the entire back wall. She walked over to the solid wood table and grazed her fingers against the finish, noting the lines she etched out of the dust that covered it. Around the table were six chairs, clearly carved out of the same wood, possibly even the same tree as the woodgrains matched. Gwen stepped into the kitchen to find that nothing had been touched since the last person left. A gas range, a round, old-school refrigerator that looked like one she had seen in movies set in WWII that they used as a bomb shelter. Brass pots and pans hung from a ladder above an island with butcher block as the countertop. The wood floors creaked with age and disuse as the women walked through.

"It doesn't even smell mousy," Betsy noted aloud. "Musty, yes, but not mousy."

"It doesn't look like any raccoons have been living here," Gwen replied.

Margo was about to go up the stairs when they heard another car drive in. The three sisters stepped back out onto the porch to see a weathered-looking man clamber out of his truck. He wore a green flannel with his sleeves rolled up, blue jeans, and leather work boots. His gray hair matched his gray mustache, which was tinged brown. Presumably from all of the cigarettes he smoked, because as soon as his gruff voice called out, they heard his deep, gristly tone. "Afternoon!" he called out. "You must be the Hampton girls." He had a slight hook in his gait as he walked up to the porch. He stretched his tan, leathery hand out to shake each of the three's hands.

"My name is Gil," he said, introducing himself. "Maury gave me a jingle the other day telling me yous all had a meeting today. I had a feeling you'd want to come out here, so I was watching for yous cars." Gil smiled a genuine smile. "Maury thought you might have some questions, so here I am."

"I'm sorry, who are you?" Margo asked. Given her all-black designer look with her arms folded and lips pursed, her body language proved how skeptical she was.

Gil laughed. "I've been keeping up the place," he said. His hands waved as he talked. "See, your Gran hired me, oh...forty years ago or so to do all the maintenance. See, I live right down the road, and once your grandad passed, your Gran asked if I could help fix things when they needed fixin'. She didn't like being out here all alone, so I'd come check on her when she came. I even mets yous when yous was little! Dropped off some old toys and schoolgirl puzzles back in the day for yer."

Gwen watched as a memory passed over Margo.

"Yes, I guess I do remember seeing you once in a while," Margo said.

"Yes, yes, that was me!" Gil smiled again. "Then before your Gran passed, bless her soul, she gave me some moneys to keep watch over the place. She didn't ask for much, just to check on it and call your mama if something happened. I never heard from your mama, but once a year I'd get a check in the mail from her. So I kept watch over the place. I come over every few months in the winter, check to make sure no water leaked in in the spring, make sure no trees came down in a summer storm, that kinda thing."

Gwen was bursting with questions. "I've never been here before," she said. "What can you tell me about it?"

Gil's eyes lit up. He scratched his chin as if figuring out where to start. "Oh, let's see," he said. "Yer grandad built this place after the Civilian Conservation Corps (CCC) disbanded in the 1940s before he went to war. He had worked for the CCC building all sorts of buildings and structures for the State Park. He bought this little piece of land on the edge of the forest, so he started building it when he got off work from the CCC. He even used leftover wood to build this here porch." Gil grazed his hands over the large wood beams. "He was a good man, your grandad. If I remember correctly, he and yer Gran got married here."

"Here?" Gwen squealed. "I didn't know that!"

"Oh yes," Gil confirmed. "Yer Grandmother's frame is upstairs in the bedroom with their wedding photo, I believe. But yer Gran, she moved to town not long after he passed. Wanted to raise her family in town, I guess. But she came out here often. Yes, she would come for holidays and practically lived out here in the summer." Gil motioned to the woods. "She even had me haul in the Christmas tree she picked out every dang year. It didn't matter that there was dang near three feet of snow!" His gristly laugh turned into a cough.

"And she paid you to keep this place up?" Betsy asked. "And then my mother continued to do so? I don't ever remember writing or sending a check up here."

"Ah. That," said Gil. "Well, once I heard about yer mama, I just took this on my own. I didn't care about no money. I knew yous be coming one day. I remember you as tots." He smiled and shook his head. "Hard to believes yous all grown up."

Gwen gave a sincere smile back. "It shows that you have taken care of this place extremely well. Thank you for loving it as much as Gran did."

Gil blushed as his hand went through his hair. "Oh, you know. It'd be a shame to let a beautiful place like this rot from the inside out," he said. "I keep the rodents out the best I can. I turn the water on every year to make sure no pipes are leaking. The propane tank has been full for years, so I don't mess with it. And I keep the electricity on. It's not much, so I just add 'er to my bill."

Margo softened and extended her hand. "Gil, thank you. You have been most helpful." She shook Gil's hand like she was in a business meeting back in Chicago. "I think my sisters and I will do some more exploring around the property and then be gone."

"Sure, sure," he replied. "Just watch the weather, though. They say a storm's passing through later and if it rains like they say it's gonna, this roadway here washes out and is impossible to get through." Gil motioned to the drive which Gwen noticed was more dirt than gravel.

"Thank you, Gil," Margo said. "I'm sure we'll be long gone before then."

"Alrighty," he said. He made his way down the steps and sauntered back to his pickup. He leaned out the window before he drove off, "Be sure to holler if yer need anythings!" And with that, he put his truck in reverse before heading out of the drive. Trees enveloped him and the sound of his truck faded.

"There is so much history here!" Gwen exclaimed. "Did you know any of this? About our grandad? About Gran?"

Betsy was quiet, looking off toward the lake. "I knew nothing," she said softly. "I feel like I don't know anything anymore."

Margo was the one who shook Betsy out of her trance by stomping her foot on the hardwood floor. "Well, let's get back to exploring," she said. "I don't want to drive back to Lansing in the rain."

With that, the three sisters trailed inside to uncover more truths about their family.

Chapter 7

Betsy and Gwen followed Margo up the steep, creaking stairs to the second floor. At the top, the beautifully carved, dark-stained banister showed wear from decades of use. Where the dust was wiped from their hands, Betsy took in the craftsmanship and reveled at how, with a bit of stain and polyurethane, the woodwork in the house could look pristine again. With each step they took, the floorboards creaked, but not from loose boards or disrepair. Betsy recalled the same groans in the same places from when she was a child running through the house.

Memories flooded back to her. Weekends spent with Gran; she and Margo played hide and seek, only to find each other when the floors noisily gave them away. As she opened up the bathroom, Betsy caught a whiff of Gran's pink bubble bath at the sight of the porcelain claw foot tub. On the wall hung two watercolor paintings she instantly recognized. There, in pastel shades of pink and yellow, were her Gran's favorite flowers, tulip lady fingers. Betsy couldn't help herself, so she gingerly opened the cabinet and gasped at the sight of the same scratchy towels they had used to dry off as children.

As she made her way down the hall, pictures of Gran and Grandad smiled at her. Betsy could hear Gran's loud, boisterous laugh as she looked through the photographs hanging on the wall. The pictures encapsulated a simpler time, of Gran and Grandad's younger years and their small family before Grandad passed. *She was so young when he died,* Betsy thought. *Two daughters and Gran took care of them all by herself.* Betsy recognized her mother right away, with a large gapped, toothless grin in the black-and-white photo, surrounded by her sister and their three dogs. She couldn't have been more than six years old. Grief plagued Betsy at the thought of losing Jake and having to raise Sam and Dani all alone.

Voices woke Betsy from her trance and she found herself in what used to be Gran's room. It still smelled faintly of her, Betsy thought. Or maybe this is how it always smelled, familiar to Betsy as a child and recognizable as an adult. The queen-sized bed took up most of the room, but it was still made up with the unmistakable, homespun, friendship star quilt that Gran made during the war.

"I needed something to do with my hands," Gran said to Margo and Betsy as children. "This is just one of the quilts I made to keep myself busy with what little fabric we had. When our clothes were too threadbare to use for rags, I couldn't bear the thought of throwing them out, so I started sewing them together. I didn't know what I was doing, but before I knew it, I sewed a blanket. So I backed it with old sheets and voila! A new blanket for my bed!" Betsy ran her hand over the quilt and was immediately transported back to her childhood, sitting on the bed listening to Gran's stories. Betsy noted the buttons on a patch from Gran's jacket, the doily collar on a patch from her dress, and a yellow gingham on a patch from a work shirt.

"Are you crying?" Gwen asked as she stood beside Betsy.

Betsy took a sizable inhale to steady herself as she reached her hand up to wipe her cheek. "This is a lot, that's all," she responded. "It's been so many years."

Margo came in and stood in silence next to her two sisters, clearly taking in the room. "It's like nothing has changed," she breathed. "It's like I never left."

Gwen turned to her two sisters and said, "Can you please tell me what's going on?" She crossed her arms as she sat on the musty bed. "I never even knew about this place and here you two are overcome by it. Obviously, this was before I was born or whatever, but someone has to explain this to me."

Margo ignored Gwen's request and walked over to the large cedar chest under the window. She pushed open the sheer drapes and the room flooded with afternoon light. She opened the window with surprising ease to let in fresh air. The shadows of the trees danced across the floor, revealing another layer of dust where they hadn't stepped yet.

"Look at this," Margo said as she opened the chest with a heave. The lid grumbled as it was lifted. Inside were photo albums and framed pictures stacked together, along with other personal items presumably belonging to Gran. As Margo lifted an album out, she paged through noting its contents. "This is Gran when she was young! Before babies, I believe."

Betsy grabbed another, "This is, too!"

Curiosity got the better of Gwen and she paced over to grab one herself. The three sisters paged through album after album, talking over one another to describe the pictures that Gran had dutifully detailed under each one. Between photo albums, mementos of Gran's life were carefully lifted out of the cedar chest and displayed on the bed between the sisters.

As the three sat around, reminiscing about their Gran's life, they hardly noticed the dark clouds rolling in until a slow, deep roll of thunder sounded. All three looked up and Gwen jumped when a sudden clap of thunder exploded in the sky along with a streak of lightning, followed by a downpour of rain.

"Oh my gosh!" Gwen jumped up from the bed and ran to the open window. "It's literally pouring outside!" She shut the window before a puddle appeared underneath it.

Betsy looked at her watch. "It's 5:14!" she exclaimed, sitting up on the bed. "We've been here all afternoon! Gwen, we have to get home!" She started piling up albums to place carefully back into the cedar chest. "Help me put this away."

Margo and Gwen bounced up at the request. Rain rattled against the window, signaling its arrival. Margo pulled up her phone to check the radar. "Ugh, there is like, no reception around here," she said. "I'll see if it's better downstairs." She turned and Betsy listened to the floors groan as she descended the stairs.

"I can't believe we lost track of time," Betsy said. She was frantic, trying to put everything away gingerly as reverence to Gran's life.

"It'll be fine," Gwen soothed. "I can drive, too, you know."

Betsy stopped and stared at her sister. "You really want either of us driving in a thunderstorm, in the middle of nowhere, on windy roads with no reception?"

Gwen conceded. "You're right," she said. "But maybe this was a good thing? You know, the three of us together? Getting lost in the moment? Laughing and remembering Gran?"

Betsy's face gave away her displeasure. "Oh, do not think this was any kind of bonding day, Gwennie-girl. This was a one-and-done thing." Betsy adjusted her height to look Gwen straight in the eye. "Do not think for one moment that we are one big happy family again!" She walked over to the window and looked out, pointing. "I'm sure she's already checking flights back to Chicago."

Gwen walked over to the window, craning her neck to see. "She wouldn't leave like that."

Both Betsy and Gwen watched as a figure ran out of the porch, a jacket held over her head until she reached the car. The hum of the engine was barely audible over the rain, but the lights gave her away.

In silence, Betsy and Gwen stared as the black BMW reversed away from the house and then proceeded to drive down the gravel driveway as the rain poured down. Just like that, the lights disappeared in the trees.

Gwen stood slowly, her breath sharp. "She just left," she said.

Betsy, eyes lit with rage, tried to calm her breathing. "Yep," she said. "That's what she does best."

Chapter 8

Rain poured down and the BMW's wipers couldn't keep up, even on high. Margo squinted through the windshield, cursing at the torrential weather. She could barely make out the road ahead of her, using the bits of illumination from the sporadic flashes of lightning. The trees rattled in the wind and shook menacingly with each clap of thunder. Margo's hands were gripped on the steering wheel; her body was tense with anxiety. The next thing she knew, a flash of lightning crashed overhead and before she could comprehend what had happened, a large aspen succumbed to the blast and collapsed right in front of her. Margo slammed on the brakes and felt the car skid down the now washed-out road before making a stop in front of the fallen tree.

Shaking, Margo sat numb. "Oh my god," she screamed, over and over again. "What just happened? I have to get back!" Margo put the car in reverse, threw her arm over the passenger's seat and looked back. It was pitch black. She couldn't see anything. She heard herself groan. "I'll never stay on the road," she said. "Now what am I supposed to do?"

Before she could talk herself out of it, she flung open the door to run back down the drive. As soon as she stood, her feet slid in the muck, soaking instantly through her favorite Fox and Geese leather shoes. Thick droplets of rain pounded against her, pelting her skin as she lurched forward. She put her arm up to shield her face as she staggered back towards the cabin. Through the thick woods, she could barely make out the outline of the house, except for the light on upstairs where she had just left her two sisters. Margo slipped, falling to the ground, covering herself completely in muck and mire. She could feel the small trenches of rainwater spilling down the drive, marking its path of a complete washout.

Margo stood, now completely drenched from head to toe, and pressed her way forward back to the house.

Breathless, she staggered in the front door to be greeted by two faces, hardened like stone.

"The road," Margo gasped. "It's washed out! And a tree! A tree...it fell right in front of my car! Lightning struck right in front of me!" She shivered as she panted, still holding onto the door handle for support. Margo looked up to Betsy and Gwen, both showing no sign of emotion.

"Where were you going?" Gwen asked.

"I...I was trying to get a signal," Margo stammered. "There's no cell service down here, so I was going out to the road."

"And then what? Were you going to come back and report that it was raining?" Gwen asked. Her sarcastic tone did not falter.

"Right," said Betsy. "Do not tell me that you didn't notice that there was hardly any cell service on the way out here. We are in the middle of the woods, Margo! Of course there's no service out here!"

"No...I, I don't know?" Margo replied. Her exasperated tone showed signs of frustration. "I don't know what I was doing or thinking. I wasn't leaving, though!"

Betsy laughed, her head cocking back. Margo winced at the cruelty of the inflection.

"You weren't leaving. Yeah right," Betsy said. "But guess what? You did leave just now. Just like you did twenty years ago! As soon as it gets hard or uncomfortable or actually? It's whenever you don't want to face the truth, you just *leave*."

Gwen shifted uncomfortably. "Bets," she said gently.

"No, this needs to happen," Betsy shouted. "I have been waiting years to get this off my chest and since I don't know when I'll ever see you again, it might as well be now." Betsy's hair tousled wildly as she spoke. Her animosity towards Margo reverberated to all corners of the room.

Margo took a deep inhale. She stood up straight, dripping water and sludge onto the hardwood floor, but she didn't back down. "And what is it that you'd like to say to me?" she asked defiantly.

That was the invitation that Betsy had been waiting for. "First of all, how could you? How could you leave me with her? I was fourteen! Fourteen years old and having to mother Gwen. But not just that, I had to mother our mother because you left! Dad was working all the time, and I was the one who had to pick up the pieces! I had to make sure Gwen was looked after! I am the one who raised her. Fed her. Made sure she did her homework and got to school on time. I'm the one who stayed up late making sure she met curfew! I helped fill out her FASFA forms and proofread her college applications. I stayed in Harrison because I *had to.* Because once Dad died, I had to help Gwen through school and off to college, and then Mom started to fail. So when I wasn't at work, I was at the house checking on her! Morning, noon, and night! I made sure she had groceries or took her meds or bathed. And when that got too hard, I moved Mom in with us. For years she lived in the front bedroom and for a little bit, it felt like she was getting better. She was able to have a conversation and remember it days later. I wasn't repeating myself nearly as much because she was doing better. Until she wasn't. Jake and I kept her living at home as long as possible. We tried, oh god, did we try. It just got to be too much. And so we brought her to Twin Pines when they had an opening in the memory care unit."

Visibly, Betsy's body language softened as relief washed over her as she continued. "And what a reprieve that was! Not to be on alert 24/7. She could have her needs met by staff who knew how to care for her." Betsy closed her eyes as the tension in her shoulders dropped. But as she opened them, Betsy glared across the room at Margo. "And still, I kept you in the loop. All the unanswered calls. The voicemails, text messages. I kept you on speed dial because I thought you should know! And obviously, you didn't care, because not once did you respond! Not once!" Rage filled Betsy once again. She took a few steps toward Margo and pointed her finger. "You have no idea how hard this has been! All of it!" Betsy pointed at Gwen but kept her eyes locked on Margo. "I raised her myself! I'm the one who figured shit out! All while you ignored us, going on with your life like we didn't exist. Moving to Chicago. Getting married without telling us. Living in a fancy highrise."

Margo's surprised expression signaled mockery to Betsy. "Oh, didn't think we knew all about that?" Betsy asked. "Of course, we knew! You of all people should know that social media never lets you keep secrets!"

Margo, albeit soaked to the bone, felt numb. Physically, mentally, and emotionally. After a lapse in the verbal barrage from Betsy, she looked up warily at the two sisters standing in front of her. "You're right," she said. Her tone was soft and sincere, for all the fight had run out of her. "You're right," she said again. "I did leave you all those years ago. I just...couldn't handle it."

Betsy scoffed again, "You couldn't handle it? Margo! I was fourteen when you checked out! I WAS A CHILD! I sure as hell couldn't handle it, but I did! Do you know why? Because I had to!"

Margo sighed. "I know," she said. "And I'm sorry. I should have been there."

"Damn right, you should have been there!"

When Margo's gaze met Gwen's, she saw a look of forgiveness. "Gwennie, I'm so sorry. I never meant to hurt you." Gwen raced over and embraced Margo, ignoring the fact that she was sopping wet.

"I knew you'd come back," Gwen whispered in Margo's hair. "I just knew you'd come back to us."

As they broke apart, Margo held onto Gwen's arms and looked into her hazel eyes. "I promise, I'll spend the rest of my life trying to make it up to you." Gwen smiled and nodded in agreement. She then turned to face Betsy, in solidarity with Margo.

"And Bets, I know my words will never make up for my actions, but I truly am sorry. I shouldn't have left. Just now in my car, but also? All those years ago. I'm sorry I didn't help you. I'm sorry I didn't see past anything outside of myself. I just knew I couldn't stick around. I guess..." Her voice trailed off. "I guess I was afraid."

Betsy folded her arms and stood just like she had as a disgruntled teenager. Margo smiled at this recognition. "I don't hate you, even though I want to," Betsy said.

"That's why I kept reaching out. Because I knew deep down you'd want to be a part of our family. Or that's what I hoped."

Margo reached for Betsy. "Thank you," she said as she took Betsy's hand. "I have always wanted to be your family. I just didn't know how to be. And after so much time had passed, I didn't know how to reach back out. It was easier to ignore than to dive back into the thick of it."

Margo watched Betsy's shoulders relax and her eyes soften. "I'm not saying I forgive you," she said. "But I do feel better."

Margo laughed. "Well, can I at least get a towel and dry off a bit? The rain hasn't let up and there is still a tree blocking the drive, so it looks like we're going to be here for a bit."

Gwen disappeared and when she came back, she had two towels in her hand. Margo recognized them instantly from her childhood. Her heart squeezed with nostalgia.

"I think I saw firewood on the back porch," Betsy said. "Maybe I can get a fire going. I also have a bag packed in the back of the van for a change of clothes."

Betsy and Gwen both looked at Margo. "And since I'm already soaked, I guess I'll go get it." She chuckled, "I promise I'll be *right back!*" She turned to the door and slipped into the rain once again.

It wasn't long before Betsy had a roaring fire going, Gwen had found some tea in the cupboards (only expiring two years ago) and Margo had her hair up in a towel, wrapped in a quilt from upstairs and wearing Betsy's extra clothes underneath. As the three sisters held their mugs gingerly, steam rising, Gwen asked gently, "Now can you tell me about this place?"

Margo and Betsy looked at each other. "Go ahead," Betsy said. She sank back into the sofa that she had just pulled the bedsheet off of. As she did the same to the rest of the furniture, nostalgia for summers and holidays with Gran overtook her.

"You'll have to fill in anything I miss," Margo said to Betsy. She lifted one foot to the couch, wrapped her arm around her knee, and faced Gwen. "So, we used to come here when we were little. Mom would bring us out every so often, but I mostly remember coming up here with Gran. She'd take us for close to a week, about maybe...once a month?" She looked to Betsy who nodded in agreement. "And we would swim all day, ride the old bikes down the driveway as fast as we could, take baths in the big tubby upstairs. Gran would fill it with pink soap that made a ridiculous amount of bubbles."

Betsy laughed at the memory. "I smelled the soap as soon as I walked into the bathroom today!"

Margo smiled. "Gran would tell us stories about living out here and how much she missed it when she went back home to Harrison. I remember asking why she didn't live here instead, and she always said, *'Because part of the magic is being here with you.'* I just assumed she didn't want to be alone."

Betsy chimed in, "Gran always let us stay up as late as we wanted. Her favorite thing to do was pick one night to sleep outside."

Gwen's face lit up. She tilted her head to one side and looked off into the distance dreamily. "Yes!" Margo agreed. "We would gather all the sleeping bags and quilts and pillows to make a bed outside. We would always argue about who was going to use the crusty old mattress under the sleeping bag, remember that?"

Betsy laughed. "You always took it!"

"I know!" Margo took a sip of her tea. "You know, now that I think about it, Gran never asked for it. She always let us fight over who would use it, but not once did she pull rank and want to use it."

"You know, you're right," Betsy said. "And she was what, in her sixties? I can't imagine sleeping on the ground with my kids right now."

"And she always had scavenger hunts for us," Margo said. "We'd wander around the in the woods looking for different wildflowers or rocks in the water or some random object she lost in the shed."

"Oh my god, that's right!" Betsy laughed. "Except for the time we found bear paw tracks. I didn't know what it was until I showed her on a walk! Gran then had us make bear traps."

"The bear traps," Margo marveled. "Old tin cans, jingle bells, spoons, and what else…pinecones? Which, saying it out loud now, I realize were basically just windchimes." She laughed at the innocence of the memory.

"This sounds amazing," Gwen said. "Why did you stop coming here? Gran obviously still came here."

A look passed between Margo and Betsy. Margo shifted uncomfortably. "Well, we came home after a week with Gran here at the cabin," she started. "You were not quite two, so that made Bets twelve, and me, sixteen. But when we came home, you were there all by yourself. It was clear that Mom had an episode that day and left, not remembering that you were home. Dad must've been gone, because that's when Gran took us for the week, when he was off working. You were crying, hungry, in a dirty diaper, and Betsy and I knew something was wrong."

"It was awful," Betsy said. "I can just see your little baby face, hungry and wanting a banana." She squeezed her eyes shut. When she opened them, she looked right at Gwen and said, "I couldn't leave you with her ever again. So I guess I made a vow to you that I would always be there, no matter what. And that's what I did."

Gwen looked sadly at her sister. "I had no idea," she breathed. "I mean, I know you practically raised me. But I didn't know it was because of this." Gwen put her mug into her lap and stared at it.

"Oh Gwennie-girl," Betsy said, leaning over and reaching for her sister's hand. "I have never once regretted being your sister or doing what it took to raise you!" She looked into Gwen's eyes and squeezed her hand. "Not once. And I would do it all over again."

Gwen's eyes filled with tears. "I wish that you didn't have to."

Betsy smiled as tears passed the brim of her eyes and fell down her cheeks. "But I did."

Margo set her mug down on the end table. "It was after that...that I kinda checked out," she continued. "I don't know, I guess I focused on what I needed to do to graduate and get out." Margo clasped her hands over Gwen's. "I'm sorry I wasn't there when you needed me. And Bets, I'm sorry I wasn't there for you, too. I was angry and young, and I don't know...wanted to prove myself somehow. So, I got the hell out, worked my ass off through college, worked my way up, and well... married an asshole, divorced said asshole, and now work too much and have no social life whatsoever."

Betsy wrapped her arms around her sisters as the couch creaked underneath them. "We all did what we had to do," she said. "I'm not saying it was right or it was wrong, but we did what we could with what we had. We were all trying to survive on our own. Maybe now we can move on together?"

Gwen and Margo laid their heads on Betsy's shoulders in solidarity. For a brief moment, the three of them were united as a front once again.

"But do we have to be so together that we have to stay like this?" Margo asked.

Gwen lifted her head as Betsy burst out laughing. "Too much togetherness?"

"I mean, it is a lot of touching," Margo laughed. She stood to find her original spot back on the end of the couch. "I can be together from over here."

The women laughed and continued to reminisce with stories of their childhood at the cabin, followed by details of their lives that they had missed. Gwen gave updates on her dating life post-college, Betsy raved about Dani and Sam growing like weeds, and Margo soaked it all in. She gave tidbits here and there about her life. Gwen was particularly interested in her marriage and divorce. That was no big deal, Margo had worked through that mess with her therapist. But there was a little niggling in the back of her mind, wanting to open up with this newfound connection. Yet she couldn't bear to.

What she didn't say out loud didn't exist.

Or at least that's what she kept telling herself.

Chapter 9

By the time morning broke, the sun filtered through the windows and Betsy awoke to her two sisters sprawled out on the couches next to her. Soft snoring came from Margo who was nestled under Gran's quilt. Betsy drank in the sound, for it instantly brought her back to her childhood as she looked around the room. She gazed over to Gwen and smiled, for she finally felt the peace in her heart she had so longed for. Betsy had always questioned if the pain and betrayal of grieving her sister who left her all those years ago or the passing of her mother would ever fade. And while the loss of her mother still resided within her, she noticed a shift within herself. A lightness, possibly a contentment, broke through and rose to the surface. *I am at peace,* Betsy thought. Always an early riser, she gingerly scooted off the couch, wrapped herself in her quilt, and padded to the kitchen.

As she opened the cupboard doors, she found old dishes, bakeware, and pots and pans, but of course, there was no food. *Nobody's lived here in ages,* she thought. Then she realized the treasure trove of snacks she had out in the vehicle. Early on in motherhood, she learned to never leave home without a supply of snacks for she never knew when she'd have to stave off hangry kids. Betsy quietly slipped outside and she stood on the front porch soaking in the sights and sounds of a beautiful fall day in Michigan.

Trees rustled in the breeze and loose leaves twirled to the ground. Honking overhead prompted Betsy to shield her eyes and look to the sky to watch a flock of geese migrating south for the winter. She watched in awe at their grace and beauty, flanked in a v-shape formation. She listened as their honks relayed back and forth, echoing on as they flew further away. Betsy inhaled deeply, aware of the crisp air entering and filling her lungs. *It feels like I can finally breathe again.* As she stepped off the porch, two squirrels jumped out from beneath her and ran off into the tree next to the house. She opened the back door of the van and it glided open at the prompt. Betsy spotted her stash of granola bars, energy bars, trail mix, and pre-portioned crackers. She grabbed the container, where she gave a silent thanks for always keeping it full for fear of being stranded in the middle of nowhere in the winter months. *Or in a storm where a tree falls and blocks our way home,* she thought. Betsy then opened the back hatch of the van which revealed half a case of bottled water and Powerade, left over from Sam's football jamboree two weeks ago. *I'm so glad I forgot to take these out with everything going on.*

Betsy quietly brought the nourishment into the cabin, only to find Gwen up rummaging through her purse. Gwen stood triumphantly with packets in her hand. "Ah ha!" she said.

"What is that?" Betsy whispered.

"Instant coffee! I always keep some in my purse," Gwen said as she smiled broadly. "You never know when you're going to need a cup!"

Betsy laughed as she held up the container of snacks. "Like this?" she said. "It's not pancakes and eggs like Gran used to make us here, but at least we won't starve."

Gwen and Betsy both looked over at a stirring Margo. She looked at herself in confusion before remembering that she borrowed her clothes from Betsy last night.

"Good morning," Betsy said.

"Yep," Margo replied.

"I'll put on a kettle," Gwen said as she took the water from Betsy's feet. "I'd rather be safe than sorry, so bottled water it is. Coffee will be ready in a few!"

"Mmmhhmmmm," Margo said.

"Still not a morning person?" Betsy asked.

"Not until about 10:00 a.m.," Margo replied. "What time is it, anyway?"

Betsy looked at her watch. "8:11."

"Figures," Margo said. "What time did we fall asleep last night?

"The last I looked, it was after 2:30," Betsy said.

"So coffee is definitely in order. I went out to the car and found some snacks. We have a decent amount, but who knows when we'll get out of here, so we'd better ration it."

"I don't eat breakfast anyway," Margo said as she stood. "Just coffee." She made her way to the bathroom.

~~~

After her coffee woke her up a bit, Margo said, "Well, I'm going to walk up the drive to see what the rental looks like. The last thing I need is to be charged for damage because it was sitting outside during a thunderstorm."

"I think I'm going to explore more around the property," Betsy said. "I want to see what I remember and if anything's changed."

"Do you want me to go with you up the drive?" Gwen asked. Her eager tone made her sound like a tag-along kid again.

"No, why don't you go with Betsy," Margo said. "I'm sure it's fine. I'll just meet up with you in a bit."
~~~

Gwen tried to hide her disappointment, but Margo spotted it before it flashed away. Soon she found herself trekking alone up the drive in her still-soaked leather shoes, teetering around the puddles and spongy spots. As she approached the black BMW, she couldn't spot any visible signs of damage. She made a lap around the vehicle, mentally noting that everything looked sound. "Thank god," she muttered. The interior light sprung on, and the door dinged three times as she opened it. Margo sat in the driver's seat and laid back on the headrest. Her body relaxed into the leather seats where she closed her eyes and breathed. After a few moments, she opened her eyes and pulled out her phone where she powered it back on. *Still no bars,* she thought. Margo turned the key in the ignition and in doing so, the hotspot appeared. *I can connect to Wi-Fi in the car! Of course!* Margo turned her Bluetooth on, connected to the Wi-Fi and a day's worth of missed notifications started pinging in her hand.

"Oh my god," she said, revolted. She watched in horror as emails pulled through, missed text messages from her team piled in, and voicemails popped up. She scrolled through her email, not opening a single message, but mentally tallying what awaited her when she returned to the office on Monday. They knew she had taken a long weekend for personal reasons, but the work didn't stop just because Margo wasn't in the office. Her team knew she liked to be in the loop. Margo then looked at missed calls. In red, she saw a familiar number. At 1:52 p.m. yesterday, she had a missed call from her doctor's office. When she tapped on the voicemail button, she read the first two lines of the transcript while a voice quietly played its message.

"Hello, Ms. Graham. This is Roni, Dr. Abram's nurse. We are trying to schedule that biopsy…"

Margo stopped the message and pressed the side button to turn off the phone. She still grimaced every time she heard her married name, knowing she had been meaning to change it ever since the divorce. Margo closed her eyes and rested her head back against the seat again. She lifted her hands to rub her eyes and her face, willing for time to both stand still and to reverse.

Margo felt grateful for the breakthroughs she and her sisters had made in the past twenty-four hours, but also, Margo longed to go back to six months ago when her mother was still alive, she was busting her back to land her major client, and she was blissfully ignorant of the lump in her left breast.

It was just six weeks ago that she was in her doctor's office. Three weeks before that, Margo was in the shower when she noticed a small bump. It was on her left side, between her armpit and her breast. *What is this?* As her fingertips massaged over it, she tried to decide if she was really feeling something or if it was her imagination. For one second, she could feel something, and the next, it was gone. *Lumps don't normally move around,* Margo thought. In everything that she has read, women know when they find a lump. But Margo didn't know. The following nights as she showered after the gym, Margo kept massaging the left side, willing for something to be there. After consulting Doctor Google and thinking back to her previous annual appointments, Margo determined that it was just dense breast tissue and there was nothing to worry about. Besides, she just turned thirty-eight. She was too young to have breast cancer. To be on the safe side, she scheduled her annual visit with her primary doctor. With how busy she was at work, she thought, *three weeks will fly by.*

Her doctor scolded her for waiting to make the appointment after Margo brought up that she thought she felt a lump but wasn't sure.

"I want to get you in for a mammogram right away," Dr. Abram said as she checked Margo over.

"Do you feel a lump?" Margo asked. The sudden realization that this could be more serious than she thought hit her. A cold sweat broke down her back, making the disposable paper on the exam table stick to her body as she shifted uncomfortably.

"I'm not sure what I feel," her doctor replied. "But I don't want to take any chances. You are due for your first mammogram in two years anyway, so we will have it done a bit early. Once we have imaging, we can confirm it's dense breast tissue or focus on next steps if it's anything else."

Anything else, Margo thought. "Like cancer."

Her doctor lowered Margo's arm, shifted her gown over her shoulder, and looked Margo squarely in the eye. "We're not going there until we know more. For now, we err on the side of caution. I'll put the referral in right away."

Two days after that, Margo learned firsthand about the passage other women over the age of forty lament about; the pain from the jostling, the squishing, the contortion-like positioning to get a clear picture. As she dressed, Margo looked at her breasts in the mirror. She was struck by a wave of nostalgia remembering them in their heyday. She wondered if they turned on her for being so underappreciated back then; now they were possibly filled with cancer. She quickly turned away and threw her clothes back on.

It was a Monday morning when her doctor called her back. Margo was at work when she answered the phone. She steeled herself for what her doctor was about to say.

"I'd like to do a biopsy," her doctor said. "The

imaging was inconclusive and like I said, I'd rather be proactive and do a bit more testing. Let's find out what we're dealing with. It could be dense tissue, but it could also be a benign cyst, or we could be dealing with something malignant."

Margo couldn't muster any words. She listened, disassociated from what her doctor was telling her. They hung up with the promise that Margo would schedule the biopsy in the coming week. But Margo didn't schedule the appointment. Instead, she threw herself into work then into her spin class at 6:00 p.m., and then into a bottle of rosé at the end of the day. She didn't even bother to keep checking to feel if there was a lump. She didn't need any confirmation that there was. She already knew.

Margo stayed in her car for a long while. She was torn between running back down to the cabin to find her sisters and climbing over the tree to find anyone on the highway to get her out of there. Just then she heard a rumble and Gil's old, beat-up pickup appeared on the other side of the tree.

Gil sauntered out of his pickup and with the door still open, he spotted Margo. "Hello!" he shouted. "Wasn't expecting to see yous today! Looks like yous spent the night here, eh?"

Margo gave a slight laugh. "Yeah, we weren't great listeners to your advice, I guess," she said over the opened car door.

Gil sized up the tree that lay between both of their vehicles. "This here looks like a mess if you ask me," he said. "I don't think my chainsaw will cut through this here." He scratched his leathery face with the gray stubble on it. "Er, looks like we's needing Butch and his loader to move this biggun."

"And is Butch near here?" Margo asked eagerly.

"Well," Gil said, drawing out his response. "I'll goes and find him. Not sure if he'll be able to make it up heres tonight, still. He lives over yonder, about forty miles, you see." Gil pointed to the left. "My guess is he's workin' on a bunch of tree removal today. It was a nasty storm that rolled through last night. Power lines knocked out all over in the next two counties."

"We have power," Margo said. "We built a fire and Betsy found snacks in her van. But I'm not sure how far it'll go."

"Ah, okay," said Gil. "I'll get the missus to whip something up while I get a hold of Butch. Then I'll be back to bring it to ya and letchya know when I'll getchya out. It shouldn't be too long. Tonight, maybe. Tomorrow for sure."

"Okay," said Margo. "Thank you, Gil. If it weren't for you checking on the cabin, I would've had to wander down the road until I found someone to save us!"

Gil snorted as he laughed. "Yous'll be fine. I'll be back!" And with that, he sauntered back into his truck and Margo watched him back out before driving away.

Margo settled into the realization that they could be here for another night. She checked the time on her phone. 9:57 a.m. She had been out here longer than she realized. With that, she turned the Bluetooth off, powered down her phone, and turned the car around to drive back to the cabin to relay the news to her sisters.

Chapter 10

The three sisters found themselves in quiet contemplation over lunch, each breaking the silence with acute observations about their obscure situation. Betsy noticed how Margo seemed more reserved, but shook it off to their late night.

"I'm going to take a rest," Margo stated as she grabbed the wrappers of the snack she called lunch. "I just can't shake this sleepiness off. I think I'll go upstairs and try a bed since the couch didn't do my back any favors last night."

Betsy and Gwen looked at each other. Something felt off. They decided to grab a few more photo albums to go through. Once they had gone through Gran's early life and their mom's childhood, Margo was still upstairs on her own. That's when Betsy and Gwen decided to explore the woods around the cabin to give Margo the quiet she needed. The crisp air breathed life into their lungs as they found old trails and abandoned structures on the property. Eventually, they found their way down to the boat house nestled in the trees by the lake. The sun was getting lower in the west; light radiated off the still water, illuminating the contrasting colors of the trees that surrounded them. The sun set much earlier in the fall and although it was still mid to late afternoon, it wouldn't be long before it would be set completely.

The dock that Betsy remembered as a launch pad into the water was lifeless in the trees, not having been in the water in over a decade, she surmised. The crunch of the fallen leaves was missing as she stepped around the red, worn-down boat house that used to store life jackets, canoes, and other outdoor items Gran had amassed over the years. Instead, leaves adhered to their shoes, both of which were cemented in mud, leaves, and wet grass.

"I don't suppose anybody has cleaned this out if the cabin itself was left untouched," Betsy said. She reached for the handle. It turned, but the door didn't budge. She used her shoulder and pushed. To her surprise, after years, maybe even decades of being deserted, it popped open.

"Wow," Gwen breathed as they gingerly climbed through the doorway.

Betsy was correct in it that it was untouched after all this time. There was no electricity out here, but the sun cascaded in through the two windows and now through the open door, revealing a time capsule of Betsy's youth. Three canoes—two green and one brown—were hanging on the wall. Worn life jackets were strewn in a pile, once orange with a single striped blue strap that was now faded to peach with their gray bands dangling lifelessly. Betsy recognized the cream pedal boat that was tipped on its side against the back wall. She smiled at the thought of when she and Margo tipped it over fully clothed in the middle of the lake. When they couldn't tip it right side up, they had to swim back to shore to get Gran. Soaking wet, they took the canoes out and towed it back to shore.

"Something's been living in here," Gwen noted as she nudged an outdoor pot out of the way with her foot. It fell into what looked like debris from an overturned garbage can. Old gas cans and a garden hose lay strewn across the floor. Cobwebs crowded the unfinished corners of the small building. One of the small windows was busted out and from the looks of it, had been for quite some time.

"It's like I am twelve years old again," Betsy said. "Nothing has changed and yet, everything has."

Gwen remained quiet, observing both her surroundings and Betsy. Just as she was about to speak, Margo trekked into the doorway.

"Whoa," Margo said. "This is a blast from the past."

"Right?" Betsy replied. "Déjà vu."

A hush descended over the three before Margo broke the silence. "I've been looking for you two. When I went to check on the car, Gil happened to be checking for damage. He said he was going to talk to some guy who would use his skid loader to move the tree. He just came back to tell me the guy won't be able to come until tomorrow morning, but Gil also brought a crockpot of chili and hot cornbread for us. I told him we would be just fine until morning."

"Okay!" Betsy said. "A plan. I like it!"

"Food," Gwen purred. "I like that better!"

They exited the boat house, shutting the door behind them, and made their way back up to the cabin. Inside Betsy gathered and rinsed soup bowls and spoons for supper. As they ate, they talked about their adventures of the afternoon, speculated about Gil and his wife's life here in the woods, laughed at each other, and soaked in the familiar feeling of being together again. Betsy realized with joy that she and Margo were both letting their guards down, opening up to one another through every story told or laugh emitted.

Margo had driven her rental car back down to the cabin, parking it next to Betsy's van. She told them how she was able to connect to the car's Wi-Fi and both Betsy and Gwen took turns using it to check messages. Betsy's husband Jake was relieved to hear from her but had received her text in the middle of the night stating they were safe.

"Let's have a fire outside tonight," Gwen said. "It's too nice out to stay inside." And with that, the women hauled armfuls of wood from the back porch out to the stone fire ring down by the lake. Margo even found two of the old wood stumps that used to sit around it buried in the thicket off to the side.

Betsy came out with the quilts from the house along with the camping chair she remembered she'd left in the back of her van. "I'm so glad I was too tired to put away any of the crap from Sam's game," she laughed.

Gwen pulled out a bottle of tequila from behind her back. "Guess what I brought?" she said with a wide smile.

Margo and Betsy groaned. "Nope, not making that mistake again," Betsy replied.

"More for me, then," Gwen said with delight and helped herself to a pull.

As darkness descended, the fire crackled and danced brighter. The dry wood burned fast, popping and sizzling as smoke rose into the night sky. Conversation flowed effortlessly between the sisters. Laughter and tears peppered the stillness of the night, interspersed with the hooting of a far-off owl or a rustling of deer in the woods.

"Remember when we used to sleep out here?" Margo mused, looking up at the stars that dotted the sky. "We would beg Gran and she would always say, *'You'll know which night is the perfect night.'*" Margo sighed. "And I don't know if she watched the weather or if she had a sixth sense about those things or if she hinted without us knowing, but she was right. There was always a quiet night when the sky broke open and we'd lay awake looking for shooting stars."

Betsy smiled at the thought. "It's like she knew," she said.

"Let's do it tonight," Gwen said.

"What?" Betsy bemoaned. "You've got to be kidding me!"

"Oh, come on! I never got to experience the magic of this place," Gwen begged. "It's only been one day but look how it brought us all back together." Wrapped in quilts, the three sisters looked at each other across the flames.

Margo, who was used to the comfort of her Tempur-Pedic bed, six pillows, and down bedding was already feeling the effects of sleeping wonky on a couch the previous night. She hesitated, not daring to let her little sister down.

"Please," Gwen asked, using a whiny tone like she did when she was young. She didn't do it very often, Betsy remembered, but when she did, it was because Gwen wanted something. Most often, Betsy gave in.

"I don't have an air mattress in the back of my car," Betsy teased. "This would be on the ground, in the cold. Us in *nature*." She used her hands to dramatize the effect.

"I'm okay with that!" Gwen said, enthusiastically. "Margo? You in?"

Margo thought back to her voicemail from earlier and then looked at both of her sisters. Their faces lit up by the fire, she could see the warmth and love that was kindling.

"I'm in," Margo said.

It wasn't long before all three were nestled together, three in a row, under the stars. Betsy had found a thin eggshell foam mattress in an upstairs bedroom and lined it with towels and a king-sized quilt. Then she layered three sleeping bags, with more blankets on top, making a cozy haven in the same spot as Gran did over twenty years before. "Believe me," she once said. "I've scoured the property, and this is the best spot."

It took some adjusting and wiggling, followed by more laughter and fits of giggles, but soon all three sisters were settled in. The stillness of the night mirrored the quietness of the sisters. Echoes of the night became clearer, along with the lull of the lapping waves hitting the shore. Constellations broke through the clouds with more dots appearing as the night pressed on.

"Do you think Mom and Gran are up there watching us?" Gwen asked quietly, her gaze still up at the stars.

Betsy replied after taking a few moments. "I hope so," she said. "I'd like to think Mom is whole again and both she and Gran are soaking this in as much as we are."

Margo remained quiet. Memories and regret flooded her mind. She was berating herself internally for how stupid it was to miss out on Gwen's growing up or how mad she was for leaving Betsy to fend for herself. She wondered if she caused the lump in her breast because of all the things she had done wrong in her life. Tears fell down the sides of her face, landing softly in her hair and pillow.

"I'm so sorry," she whispered. "I'm so very sorry." Between shallow breaths, Margo continued, "I missed out on so much. And I left you to handle everything. And then when Mom died, well...I just couldn't bear the thought of facing it all. So I know the last thing you expected was to see me show up at the lawyer's office. And then get stuck with me, here of all places."

Both Betsy and Gwen kept quiet to let her continue.

"I don't know if I believe that Gran or Mom are watching or if they orchestrated this or what," Margo said. "But when I got the letter from the lawyer, I knew I had to come back. I didn't expect either of you to forgive me. I didn't expect to get stranded here and instantly fall back in love with it. I don't know." Margo's thoughts swirled. "But I do know I'm sorry and that I'd like to make it up to you both somehow."

Betsy, snuggled in between Gwen and Margo, found Margo's hand under all the covers and squeezed it, without saying a word. She had felt the damp tears that fell from Margo's eyes.

"When I get back to the city, I need to have a biopsy," Margo said. "I'm not sure what's going to happen, and I don't expect for either of you two to drop everything because of it. But I guess I'm telling you because I've run away from so many things for so long, and I'm ready to be done running."

Betsy turned onto her side to face Margo, who was still looking up at the sky. Gwen shifted her body and partially lay on Betsy and reached her arm out to clasp a hand on her sisters' intertwined hands.

"You don't have to run anymore," Gwen said. "We're not going anywhere." She squeezed her sisters' hands. "You're safe with us."

Betsy smiled. "You're home," she said.

Margo turned her head to face Betsy and Gwen. In the moonlight, she saw tears glistening from their eyes as well, but their faces showed empathy and compassion.

"What if we come back here every year?" Gwen asked as she settled back into her sleeping bag. "I mean, we own the place. We might as well use it."

Betsy hadn't considered this fact. "You're right," she said. "Why couldn't we make this our own?"

"And we could rent it out on Airbnb!" Gwen said enthusiastically. "Make some money off of it!"

It was Margo who pulled the reins on Gwen's enthusiasm. After a moment of quiet consideration she said, "Actually I'd like to keep it just for us. For our families, I mean. I don't want to share it with anyone else."

Betsy smiled at the thought. "I agree," she said. "A place just for us."

Epilogue

One Year Later: October

Betsy pulled in front of the cabin and shut off her vehicle but didn't get out right away. Instead, she looked through the windshield at the cabin, soaking in all the details the same way she did a year ago. While much looked the same, so much was different. Or maybe it was her that was different.

Betsy smiled as she opened the door and inhaled the crisp fall air. Before she started the task of unloading all their belongings and hauling them into the house, Betsy walked down to the water, stopped at the edge, and admired the picture-perfect autumn day: bursts of red, orange, and yellow amongst the green trees. She listened to the crows cawing away in the treetops. She spotted a little splash out in front of her as a turtle came up for air before plunging again. The golden sun glistened through the clouds, enveloping everything with a slight shimmer.

Betsy's heart was eager for this long weekend. The kids had three days off school, which meant Betsy did too. Dani and Sam were staying with Jake's parents for two days while Jake worked, then he and the kids would drive up on Friday for the weekend. From the moment she brought her family to the cabin for the first time in May, Dani and Sam fell in love.

She checked her watch. 3:32 p.m. *Plenty of time to get everything ready before Margo and Gwen get here,* she thought. The plan was for Gwen and Margo to drive up together after Margo's flight from Chicago this afternoon. Her flight got in at one o'clock, and by the time Gwen picked her up and got out of the city, it would be a good three-hour drive. Betsy hoped the trip wouldn't fatigue Margo too much. Betsy wanted everything to be perfect for their first time back at the cabin.

After starting a fire in the stone fireplace, lighting candles, and turning on a playlist of Lorie Line, Betsy got to work in the kitchen. Mushrooms and peppers sautéed while Betsy opened a quart of her homemade tomato sauce, freshly canned at the end of summer. She found a pot to boil water, clicking on the pilot light to ignite the stove. Soon, the aroma of garlic and tomatoes filled the main floor of the cabin. Betsy mentally took note of the Caesar salad dressing chilling in the fridge and the frozen garlic bread that wasn't so frozen by the time it made it to the cabin. She smiled to herself when she spotted the stack of firewood neatly piled on the back porch, compliments of Gil.

Margo, Betsy, and Gwen all agreed to take Gil up on his offer to keep watch over the cabin. They paid him handsomely, of course, thanks in part to Margo. It was her idea to invest in the property to make it come alive again. Gil was more than happy to help. He coordinated new gravel to be leveled along the driveway to stabilize it. He assisted Jake in putting the dock out over Memorial weekend. He trimmed trees, mowed the grass, spruced up the firepit area, and even hung outdoor lights on the front porch at Gwen's request. Gil was also responsible for coordinating with the local telephone company to install Wi-Fi in the cabin.

Betsy and Gwen also dedicated time and effort to restoring the cabin to its original glory, but with a more modern feel. Margo sent up her old living room furniture, so Betsy and Gwen added touches that would correspond. Jake hung an antique light over the dining room table. A smart TV hung over the fireplace. Betsy put new towels in the linen closet and new sheets on the beds. With four bedrooms—one with twin beds for the kids—everyone had their designated space. However, not once had all three sisters been at the cabin together since they first set foot on the property a year ago.

Betsy was up in the master bedroom, Gran's old room, putting her clothes into the chest of drawers when she heard a car driving in. She stepped over to the window and saw Gwen's familiar gray Ford Escape pulling in. Anxiously, Betsy waited to see Margo climb out of the car.

Last year, after Gil's friend Butch moved the tree out of the drive, the three sisters vowed that no matter what happened, they'd stick together. Margo went back to Chicago where she scheduled her biopsy. Unfortunately, Margo called to confirm their biggest fear. It was cancer.

"Invasive Ductal Carcinoma," Margo said. "Stage II."

"Stage II, that's got to be good, right?" Betsy asked. "What are the treatment options?" Margo went on to confirm her treatment plan: chemotherapy, radiation, and a partial mastectomy.

After so many conversations, Betsy knew Margo's motivation was to get back to the cabin. That night under the stars, Margo, Betsy, and Gwen vowed that they would make the time every fall to make it back up here together. And while Betsy and Gwen had enjoyed many summer evenings and weekends here, the knot in Betsy's stomach couldn't help but be anxious to make everything just right for Margo. She knew how much this place meant to her—to all of them.

Betsy padded down the stairs just as the front door opened. Gwen gently put bags down and held the door open. Margo gingerly walked through. Her hair was styled in a short pixie cut that was so becoming on her, a deep amber color that accentuated her green eyes and high cheekbones. Officially marked as having no evidence of disease, Margo was still recovering from the past year of hell. As soon as entered the room, Margo's face lit up.

Her gaze finally settled on Betsy, standing on the stairwell. Margo broke into a wide grin and met Betsy at the base of the steps, arms outstretched for an embrace.

"Welcome home," Betsy said as they let go.

Tears welled in Margo's eyes. "I've been waiting a whole year for this!" she said. "Oh gosh, wait!" She looked behind her as if she misplaced a bag. "I have something." Gwen sidestepped as Margo scurried over to open the closet by the front door. As she stood, she proudly held a handmade, wooden sign.

"I meant to have Gil hang this by the time we arrived, but life got in the way." She laughed as she turned it around. "Now it's home."

"Is that..." Betsy tried to form words but was at a loss.

Margo smiled. "I had Gil save a slab of the tree that fell and hired a local artist to create something beautiful. I knew it needed to be a permanent fixture here; the place that brought us all back together."

On the sign, it read:

Sisterwood. Established 2022.

Acknowledgments

This novella was written in partnership with Quilter's JEM and the Northwest Minnesota Arts Council. Their unwavering support and dedication to the arts made this project possible. Kim, and all the ladies at Quilter's JEM, have been a source of inspiration, fostering a creative community that breathes life into every stitch and story.

I am also deeply thankful to the Northwest Minnesota Arts Council for its commitment to cultivating creativity and providing resources that empower local artists. Their resources and encouragement have been instrumental in bringing this story to life.

I want to express my deepest gratitude to my husband and children. Your love and support have been my greatest motivation. A special thanks to my family and friends for their love and encouragement, and to the readers who have embraced this story. Your enthusiasm fuels my passion for writing.

Lastly, to every quilter whose artistry shapes the fabric of our communities—this is for you. Thank you for weaving your stories into our lives.